# DESMOND PUCKET

### AND THE Cloverfield Junior High Carnival of Horrors

**Other books by Mark Tatulli**

# DESMOND PUCKET
## AND THE Cloverfield Junior High Carnival of Horrors

Andrews McMeel
Publishing®

a division of Andrews McMeel Universal

# 1 BACK IN THE SADDLE

The first day of school always feels so weird. It's especially weird when you're going back to the same school, just moving up a grade. It's like living in some *Twilight Zone* version of your own life from three months ago.

Maybe I'm just weirded out by this goofy first-day-of-school outfit Mom got me. Nothing says "lame" like a sky-blue sweater-vest. The good news is, I'm only wearing it once. Tomorrow it's back to basic black.

As we all stand around in our dorky new clothes waiting for them to let us in, I look around at how much some of the kids changed since I saw them in June.

The bell rings and everybody crushes toward the open doors.

Well, not really a bell sound. More like a buzzer. Like speaker feedback, or a robot scream. I have a feeling that in the front office, there's this thing:

Everybody heads to homeroom. As usual, I'm with the P's, the R's, and the Q's. I want to be with the S's, but there are so many S's that they get their own homeroom. Ricky and Becky are in the D's homeroom down the hall. Scott Seltzer is next door with the S's, and he totally doesn't deserve it. I wish my last name started with an S. Then I'd be next door, too.

With Tina Schimsky.

3

OK, OK, I admit it. I still have a thing for Tina Schimsky! I can't help it! But can you blame me?

Yes, I like Becky a whole lot, too! Becky is a great pal and she always comes through in a pinch. And going with Becky on that last ride of the Mountain Full of Monsters was awesome. But Tina . . . she's this whole other kind of magical! I guess my first real mondo-crush is sort of hard to let go of, you know?

OK, I get it. I'm wishy-washy! Give me a break! I'm still trying to figure out this whole girl thing. It can make even a hardcore Monster Magician like me sort of loopy.

The buzzer bell buzzes its annoying buzz and everybody sits. Mrs. Master then starts to hand out class schedules. I hope I don't have gym first.

Mrs. Master passes me my schedule and I look it over quickly. Language Arts. Science. French. P.E. (Whew! Fourth period.)

L.R.C. is short for Learning Resource Center, or as I like to call it: "Nap Heaven." It's really a pretty decked-out library with tons of books and computers, and it has these great cubbies for private study.

And triple period is the extra-long class that happens during the lunch periods, so having L.R.C. triple period is like a gift from the Gods of Lazyland!

Once again the robot buzzer screams and we head out to find our first class. I meet Becky and Ricky in the hall and we compare schedules.

"We better get moving, Desmond," Becky says. "Our language class is all the way in the 700 wing."

"I've got math," Ricky says with a gagging face. "I'll see you guys later."

"Let's cut through the sixth grade," I say to Becky. "It will be a lot faster."

"Seventh graders aren't allowed in the sixth grade halls."

"We're just taking a shortcut! Don't be such a chicken!"

We bolt by the lockers and duck into the sixth grade hallways. It seems like forever ago that we were last here, even though it has been only three months, and I feel oddly out of place. Well, we're almost near the 700 wing now. Just around this corner and—

"Whoa! That is the biggest sixth grader I've ever seen," I gasp. "Like, Museum-of-the-Weird big!"

"See, I told you I had a bad feeling about coming this way," Becky says as she picks up my notebook. "C'mon, let's just get out of here."

We cross into the **700** wing and head in the direction of our first class, but I can't stop thinking about the run-in with that sixth grade gorilla boy. There's something familiar about that kid . . . and he might be just the beast I'm looking for!

# 2 FIRST CLASS

"See, Becky, I'm standing there in front of the cage with the wild yeti thing, only I'm standing too close, see . . . and his arm reaches through the bars . . ."

"... THEN HE GRABS ME AND RIPS MY FACE OFF!"

"So then I'm stumbling around with just a skeleton head and fake blood is flying everywhere!"

"Uh-huh," says Becky, obviously fascinated.

"And while everyone is screaming and going nuts, the creature starts rattling the bars and suddenly the cage breaks apart and he charges into the crowd and . . ."

"Hold it, Desmond. This is what you're planning for the Carnival of Horrors?"

"Well, yeah, just the outside part."

"Principal Badonkus will never go for it. This isn't anything like your Monster Magic show."

IT'S TOO GROSS AND BLOODY!

"But, see, this is just the thing that will get people hooked," I say. "Then they'll want to go in my haunted house, where the *real* scares are—"

Suddenly the door slams and the teacher heads to the front of the classroom.

"I am Mr. Oblio and this is Language Arts II, Creative Writing. If you are in this class in error, please notify your counselor *after* you leave."

Just then the door handle jiggles and in walks . . . a *vision*!

"Second year in this school and she still gets lost. A true sign of genius," Becky says with much rolling of eyes.

"Ah, Ms. Tina Schimsky, yes?" Mr. Oblio says, looking at his roll call sheet.

"Yes," she says as she slips into the seat behind me, then whispers, "Hey, Cousin Eerie."

I snicker. Becky rolls her eyes. "Cousin Eerie" is sort of Tina's pet name for me. She got it from an old horror comic book that she found at a garage sale and said it reminded her of me.

Meanwhile, Becky, who is watching me watch Tina, is going for an eye-rolling record.

"Tina Schimsky? Do you have a brother named Keith?" asks Mr. Oblio.

"Ugh, yes, unfortunately."

"Really? I always thought him quite clever! I had him when I taught at Wood Hook Elementary."

"Well, you might get him again, Mr. Oblio. He's in sixth this year."

"I hope so. Quite clever, that one."

I remember Keith, too, and I shudder. After he ruined Tina's birthday campout in July, Keith got in buckets of trouble with his parents. Nobody saw him for the rest of the summer.

Mr. Oblio tugs on the bottom of the map and up it rolls, revealing the chalkboard beneath.

Many groans and ughs from the class.

"Yes, children, you've done it a hundred times . . . or at least five or six. But here's the trick: *this* time, I want you to do it in a totally original way; I want you to think outside the box and write and create this assignment in a way you never have before!"

Silence. And then, Troy Hooper . . .

Mr. Oblio pauses and then says:

"What is the difference between Shel Silverstein and Jeff Kinney? Or Stephen King and Dr. Seuss?"

"I don't know. They each write different, I guess," says Troy. "But how should *I* write it?"

"Exactly!" says Mr. Oblio. "How *should* you write it?"

More silence. And some "huh's?"

I raise my hand.

"Yes, Mr. Pucket?"

CAN I DO A GRAPHIC NOVEL?

"*Thank you*, Mr. Pucket!" says Mr. Oblio and he seriously looks like he's about to cry. "You MAY do a graphic novel!"

Yes! This is going to be the coolest assignment ever, even if it is a school thing.

"And incidentally, Mr. Pucket, nice sweater-vest."

# 3 THE CUULEST ASSIGNMENT EVER

Hello, lucky readers! I'm Desmond Pucket and this is my first graphic novel!

Well, first graphic novel that I ever turned <u>in</u> at school. I've written and drawn <u>tons</u> of comics at school, but that's another story!

I'm pretty famous around here for being a Master of scaring people!

make my own fangs

I have my own logo...

DESMOND PUCKET
"Gourmet of Gore"

and my own company for scaring kids!

But, wait, I'm getting ahead of myself...

...it all started with my favorite haunted ride

THE MOUNTAIN FULL OF MONSTERS!

CRAB SHELL PIER

Time: Beginning of the summer...

Holy turds! Desmond, look at this!

Mountain Full of Monsters ride closing end of summer!

Best friend, Ricky DiMarco

We can't save the ride, but maybe we can save the monsters that are inside the ride!

Idea

Of course, not everybody was sorry to see that the Mountain full of Monsters ride was closing...

That ride is an eyesore...

MR. NEEDLES, School Disciplinarian, always out to get me!

and scaring people isn't funny!

My dad's demolition company is going to blow it up! Tee-Hee!

EL JERKO, Scott Seltzer

Maybe we can charge kids money to scare other kids...

genius with electronics, BECKY DeNICKY

Ricky

...and then we can use the money to buy the monsters!

19

AND SOON

My new MONSTER MAGIC SCARING COMPANY was a huge success!

It seemed like everybody had a brother or sister to scare!

we were so busy we had to have extra help!

That's how we ended up with KEITH SCHIMSKY!

Heh Heh Heh

10 Years old and full of TERROR →

we scared kids all summer and finally we thought we had enough $ $ $...

Moolah

$374.74

Sorry, kid. I need more cheddar... like 500 bucks.

...then I'll let you take as many monsters as you can carry.

MR. HUMPHRIES, guy who runs CRAB SHELL PIER →

...but you only have three days to raise the money before I sell the monsters to the junk man!

Dang.

Moolah

Tina Schimsky is having a big campout birthday for all the sixth graders...

...I bet we can raise the rest of the money there!

Becky was right! So many kids wanted to scare their sixth grade sisters...

...that we easily raised the rest of the $500!

And so we planned a simple scare that wouldn't ruin Tina's birthday...

because Tina is sweet & beautiful and deserves the best! → Tina

Becky, queen of the eye-rollers

But the nefarious Keith had other plans...

extra points for big word

Heh Heh

...and when it came time for the scare to start, Keith pulled THE DOCTOR SHOCK✳

crazy Keith

Giant killer clowns with chain saws

✳ The ultimate scare - only for teenagers and other deserving jerks.

See, Keith doesn't get it! Scaring should leave the person breathless and laughing! Like they just went on a rollercoaster! It should be FUN!

A public Service Message

Keith wants people to cry and have nightmares! And that's a no-no! He's giving us Frightologists a bad name!

21

So anyway, Tina's Campout got so out of control that the pank rangers showed up!

And I was nabbed by the head park ranger— Mr. NEEDLES!

GOTCHA, PUCKET!

even more annoying in Shorts!

GUH!

Then Mr. Needles told me how he used to go out with my mom & how my dad scared him away!

You Puckets are all alike! You love to scare people!

And I Shall have my revenge!

Pank ranger

My dad's a dentist. The only thing scary about him is the drill.

So eventually my sister Rachel and her boyfriend Kyle the bus kid rescued me from Needles (and his stories)...

and we drove to CRAB SHELL PIER

...we gave the money to Mr. Humphries, and now I'm the proud owner of a bus load of mummies, Zombies, giant spiders, vampires, mole people, ghosts, goblins, skulls... you get the idea.

Luckily, Ricky's grandparents let me store the monsters in their giant shed...

...but I keep a couple of my favorites in my room!

Then The Seltzer Demolition company did what Scott said they would do...

mc   Ricky   Becky

BOOM!

...and that's how we ended our summer-- watching the MOUNTAIN FULL OF MONSTERS come down!

And now here's my favorite part of these stories...

WHERE ARE THEY NOW?

Mr. Humphries built a new giant roller coaster where the Mountain Full of Monsters was

$ $ $
$ $
$ $

and he's hoping next summer will be HUGE for CRAB SHELL PIER.

After Keith Schimsky ruined Tina's birthday Campout, his parents sent him to military camp for the rest of the summer.

My sister Rachel broke up with Kyle the bus kid, but she still lurks on his FACEBOOK page.

Oh, Kyle, you are such a dweeb!

She now spends her time trying to build followers on INSTAGRAM.

The last time I saw Mr. Needles, he was eating our dust as we drove to CRAB SHELL PIER!

CORSE YOU, DESMOND PUCKET!

I don't know -- where IS he NOW?!

Becky, Ricky, and I still run the MONSTER MAGIC SCARING COMPANY, where we scare kids for fun and profit...

WHOOPIE

... and NEVER to be mean!

And the monsters get pulled out every now and then for this and that...

THE END?

...but they are waiting for their BIG DEBUT at this year's CLOVERFIELD JR. HIGH CARNIVAL OF HORRORS!

# 4 THE CLUVERFIELD JUNIOR HIGH CARNIVAL OF HORRORS

I guess I should explain what this is. Every school has a carnival or fair, usually in the springtime. You know, with lame games and snack tables and it's all run by teachers who look kind of grumpy because, let's face it, they don't want to be at school on a Saturday any more than we do.

Saturday is my official Netflix binge-watching day.

CUP cakes $1.00

Mr. Ryan, (Social Studies) Not Happy

But it's safe fun and we hang around for 20 minutes and buy a Rice Krispie Treat and toss a ring in the ring toss game and in the end everybody is happy and it raises money for the school. And it's the same lame thing every year. That's how it used to be at Cloverfield Junior High, too. But that changed about five years ago, when Principal Badonkus came to town.

Principal Badonkus likes to shake things up and when she saw that the spring carnival was dull and not really making much money, she decided she had to do something.

So she came up with the idea of a Halloween-themed carnival . . .

**CLOVERFIELD JR. HIGH SCARE FAIR**

Well, that's what they called it at first. Doesn't really "sing," does it? That first year was sort of slow and everyone thought the name was kind of babyish, so they renamed it the Carnival of Horrors. After that it really took off.

Especially since they added something new: the Haunted Cafetorium!

Makes total sense, right? I mean, Lord knows what monsters are living in those garbage cans.

It sure smells like death!

Hey!

Every year a group of students converts the cafetorium into a walk-through haunted house! One kid is picked to be the leader and the whole group spends the month of October making the cafetorium even scarier than the mixed vegetables usually make it. The Haunted Cafetorium became the centerpiece of the carnival . . .

The carnival is now so popular that people come from all over to see the costumes and the parade, and go in the Haunted Cafetorium. And all of the money raised goes right into our library, Principal Badonkus's favorite part of the school. And we have the best one around; so great, in fact, that it has its own special name, the Learning Resource Center, because "library" just wasn't awesome enough to describe it. And we've got the best librarian around to run it, too: the amazing Ms. Ruebbles.

I call her "amazing" because she can remember every book a kid checked out just by looking at him!
Pucket, D... when are you bringing back "FAMOUS MONSTERS & SCARY ALIENS OF FILMLAND"?

Anyway, I've been coming to the Carnival of Horrors since it was called the Scare Fair! Last year, my first year at Cloverfield, Brent Dungler was in charge of the Haunted Cafetorium. And the captain of the A/V club and I have very different ideas of what makes a frightening haunted house effect . . .

Look at this! Is there anything scarier than evil Kirk from "The Enemy Within," Season 1, Episode 5 of "STAR TREK"?
Uh... wait, what?
me, confused
evil Kirk dummy
Brent Dungler, A/V club

But this year, I'm going to ask Principal Badonkus if I can be in charge of the Haunted Cafetorium! And I've been drawing up plans every chance I get (mostly during class).

Which is exactly what I'm doing in Language Arts when Mr. Oblio hands back our "What I Did This Summer" projects.

Hey! Not too shabby for a first-time graphic novelist! But it was the note on the last page that really made me swallow my fangs . . .

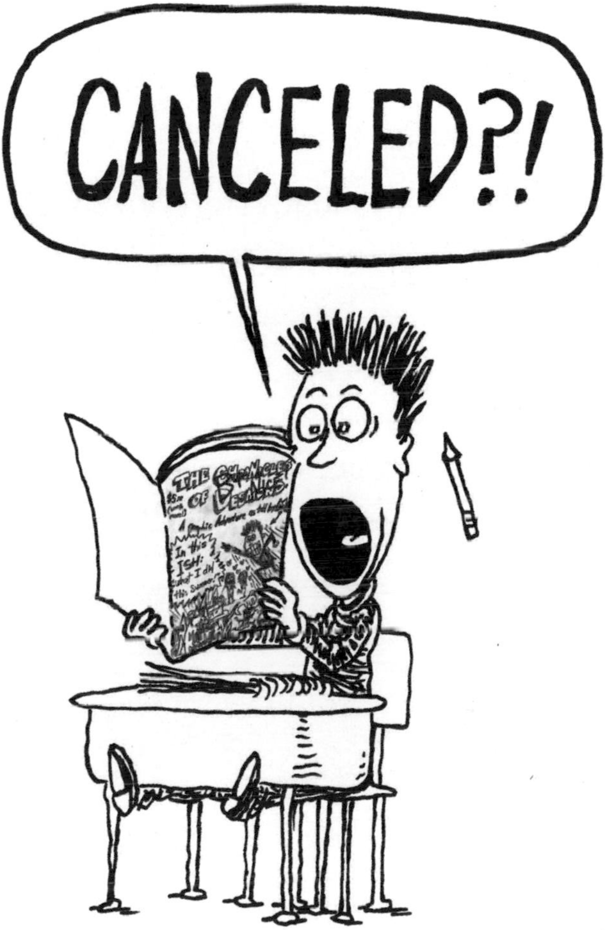
CANCELED?!

# 5 THE FOOTNOTE OF DOOM

This can't be! My mouth starts to shape all kinds of words of protest, but nothing comes out. I raise my hand but then—

—the robot buzzer screams and the pandemonium of changing classes begins.

"Wait, Mr. Oblio," I shout over the din, waving my graphic novel project wildly to get his attention.

"After school, Mr. Pucket," he says, already out the door. "You know where to find me."

I'm still in shock. Maybe I misread it. I open my graphic novel to the last page, to the footnote written in blood red ink. The footnote of doom.

That can't be true! Where did he hear that?! I can't wait until after school to find out! I have to ask Mr. Oblio what this means.

I go to science period but I can't focus. Normally the talk about asteroids on a collision course with Earth would interest me, but all I can think of is that

note. It's the same thing in every class. French. P.E.
I get hit in the face so many times playing dodgeball
that the teacher offers me a hockey mask. But I can't
think. And between classes I have one mission:

But then, as I'm heading to L.R.C. for triple
period, it hits me like a thunderbolt . . .

Of course! The Carnival of Horrors is her baby!
She invented it! Principal Badonkus will know what the
real story is.

I turn on my heel and head the opposite way, where the main offices are and—

**WHAM!** Right into that same sixth grade wall of flesh.

Who is that kid?! Well, no matter, I've got a job to do. I scramble to my feet and hustle over to the principal's office.

I decide to sneak my way in. I just have to talk to Principal Badonkus for a second. I nonchalantly stroll toward the door . . .

And then, quick as a Jedi Knight after three double-espressos, I pull the door to the office open and I slip inside.

The back of the chair is facing me and it squeaks and groans as it slowly turns around . . .

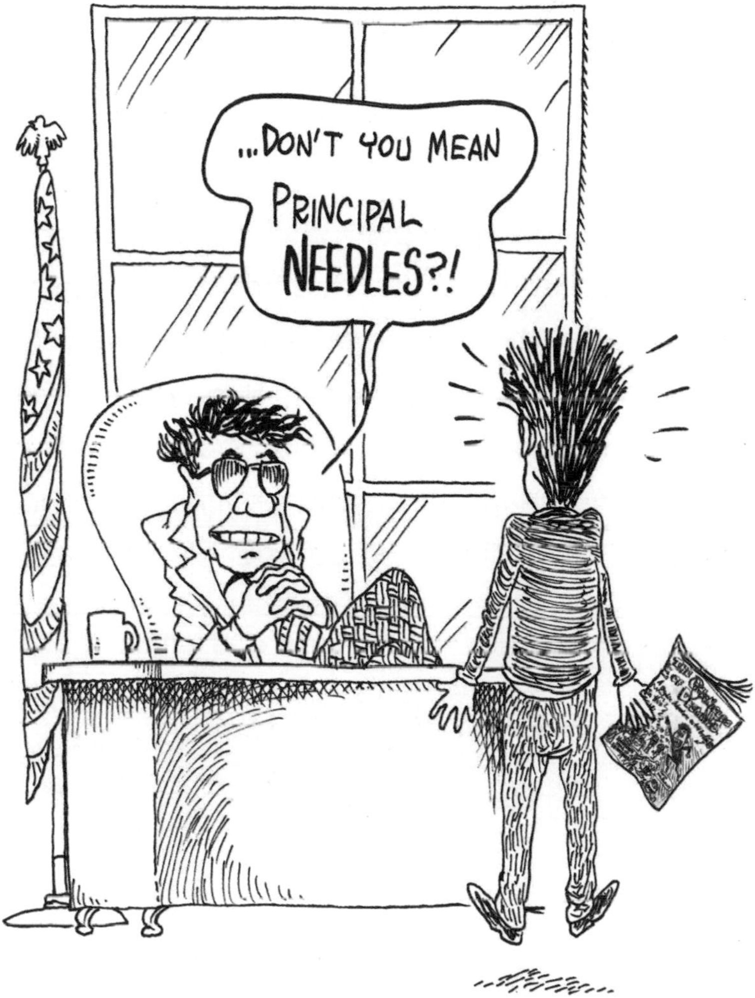
...DON'T YOU MEAN PRINCIPAL NEEDLES?!

# 6 THE PRINCIPAL IS MY PAIN

"Surprised, Mr. Pucket?"

Am I surprised that Mr. Needles is principal? Yes. Surprised he still hasn't trimmed his nose hairs? No.

"I can tell you are," Mr. Needles continues, bouncing in his creaky chair. "Well, our dear Principal Badonkus is now *Superintendent of Schools* Badonkus, and she very kindly selected me to be the new principal!"

ISN'T THAT, LIKE YOU KIDS SAY, "THE BOMB"?

THIS IS **ONE** KID WHO WON'T BE SAYING **THAT** ANYMORE.

"So, as you might guess, there's going to be some changes around here . . . the first being the end of that Carnival of Horrors!"

"Mr. Needles, you can't—"

"*Principal* Needles, if you please," he growls. "And don't think for a moment you can tell me what to do. This is my school now and I intend to straighten things out. For the best. You see that sculpture right next to you, Mr. Pucket?"

"That is J.J. Cloverfield, the founder of this school," says Mr. Needles proudly. "He's also my personal hero!"

"I can see where you get your frown," I say, peering closely at the plaster face.

"Mr. Pucket, do you know what J.J. Cloverfield's favorite saying was?"

"'I wish I had a body to go with my head'?" I ask.

Then Mr. Needles points right in my face.

"And YOU, Mr. Pucket, with your constant shenanigans and hijinks, disruptith the class!"

"J.J. Cloverfield and I will not stand for it. This is an institution of learning, not scaring!"

"But, Mr. Nee—, I mean *Principal* Needles, if—"

"I think we're done here, Mr. Pucket. Mr. Schimsky, will you please escort Mr. Pucket to his next class?"

And then, out of the shadows steps—

So this is the answer to the mystery of the extra-large sixth grader! Keith Schimsky!

"Dude! You got *ginormous*!"

"Growth spurt. Maybe it was the food at the military school."

I immediately start to think that Keith would be the perfect wild yeti monster for my opening scare idea . . . and then I remember there isn't going to be any opening scare idea or wild yeti monster because there isn't going to *be* any Carnival of Horrors! And then I snap.

"Yes, that is an old expression, Pucket. And one we don't need anymore. Now we have spell-check."

Principal Needles bends his head back to his paperwork.

"Get him outta here, Schimsky."

"And what's this?" I ask Keith as we make our way down the hall. "I don't need you to walk me to class! I know where the L.R.C. is!"

"I just do what I'm told," Keith says.

"So, what? Did Principal Needles brainwash you? Are you his goon? Did he put one of those Ceti eels in your head and now you have to do what he says?"

"A Ceti *what*?"

"A Ceti eel, from *Star Trek II: The Wrath of Khan*. They're these mind control worms that—forget it."

"No, it's nothing like that," says Keith. "Principal Needles is sort of my mentor now."

"Mentor? You mean, like an advisor? Like he's training you? For what, the Dark Side of the Force?"

Jeez, I *am* turning into Brent Dungler.

"I don't think you get it, Desmond . . ."

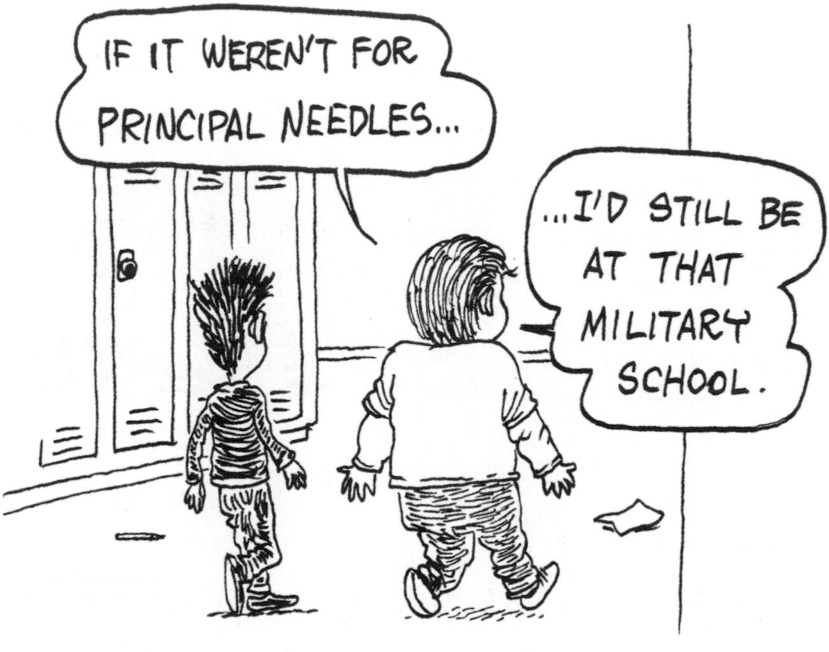
IF IT WEREN'T FOR PRINCIPAL NEEDLES...
...I'D STILL BE AT THAT MILITARY SCHOOL.

# 7 KEITH'S STORY

As soon as we leave Mr. Needles's office, Keith slips back into the creep-mode that I remember.

"Shee-zoo, Pucket, will you ever forget it? That was some scare we pulled off!"

WHOA, DUDE, THAT WAS *YOUR* SCARE! AND TOTALLY OVER THE TOP! I *KNEW* THAT WAS TROUBLE!

"Yeah, you got that right," said Keith. "When my dad found out I ruined Tina's party, he blew a biscuit!"

"Don't you mean he 'blew a gasket'?" I ask.

"No, he was eating at Dikki's Chicken Shack, choked on a biscuit, and just blew it all over."

Oh, brother.

"My dad's a house painter now, but he's also ex-military," continues Keith. "So he knows a lot of guys in the business. That's how I got shipped off to Camp Jackboot."

Keith goes on to tell me all about his summer military school experience . . .

Yeah, definitely doesn't sound like a day at the pool.

"But once I got into the routine, things seemed kind of OK and I even made some friends."

AND THEN, ONE NIGHT, WE HAD A CAMPOUT! THERE WAS A FIRE AND MARSH-MALLOWS AND WE STARTED TELLING STORIES...

". . . and I figured I'd pull out one of my ghost stories because those are really the only stories I know by heart. So I started telling 'Bloody Boots.' You know that one?"

I nodded. Every Professor of Frightology with a Master's in Monsters knows that one.

SO I START TO TELL IT, SEE, ABOUT THE YOUNG ARMY SERGEANT WHO FINDS A PAIR OF BLOODY BOOTS...

... AND HE DOESN'T KNOW WHAT TO DO WITH THEM, SO HE STICKS THEM IN A BARRACKS FOOTLOCKER.

"And then, that night, after it's lights out and all the soldiers are asleep, the sergeant hears the boots trying to get out of the footlocker! And then the next night, too, only this time, he hears the boots bust out and hit the floor!"

47

I peek at Keith and start to see that faraway, out-of-control look come into his eyes. It's the same look I saw that night when he pulled the ultimate Dr. Shock scare at Tina's birthday party. Well, Keith is a scare genius, and all geniuses are a bit whack-a-doodle-doo.

"So the sergeant says, 'That does it!' and he puts this heavy Army-issue lock on the footlocker so the boots can't possibly get out! And he goes to bed, sure that he stopped those old bloody boots for good."

Keith reaches out and halts me because we're getting close to the L.R.C.

"So I go on," says Keith. "That night, once again, the sergeant hears the footlocker struggle and bump. And he thinks, *yes, the lock is holding*!"

"But then, he hears a jolt, and the sound of the two boots hitting the wood floor! Boomp, Boomp! Then the boots get closer. Boomp, Boomp! And closer. Boomp, Boomp! Boomp, Boomp! And closer. Boomp, Boomp! Boomp, Boomp! Boomp, Boomp! Now they're right outside his door! Boomp, Boomp! And—"

"Then I flipped up my flashlight onto an old pair of boots that I had put just outside of our circle and, well, that's all it took . . ."

"The guys freaked out! Crashed through the fire. Dang near burned the whole camp down! It was a big mess and after that, nobody wanted to be my friend."

THE GENERAL CALLED MY DAD—SAID I WAS "INCORRIGIBLE," AND I NEEDED TO WORK ON MY "PEOPLE SKILLS."

OOOOOO. "INCORRIGIBLE." I'VE HEARD THAT WORD BEFORE. I STILL DON'T KNOW WHAT IT MEANS.

"Then the general told my dad that they would need more time to straighten me out, maybe even a couple years. So Dad came out to the military school, all ready to sign me up for a big long stay! I was so scared! I hated that place and now I had no friends!"

AND THEN SOMETHING MIRACULOUS HAPPENED...

... MR. NEEDLES SHOWED UP AND SAVED THE DAY!

"Mr. Needles?!" I ask. "What was he doing at your military school?"

"Mr. Needles always comes to the camp at the end of the summer. He hires cadets to do yard work at Cloverfield just before the new school year starts."

"And he hired you to mow lawns and stuff?"

"Wow, that's the first nice thing I ever heard of him doing," I say. "Are you sure it wasn't some alien version of Mr. Needles?"

"Talk to him about what?"

"Talk to him about bringing back the Carnival of Horrors!"

"Principal Needles saved me from having to go to military school! I owe him! Scaring is over for me!"

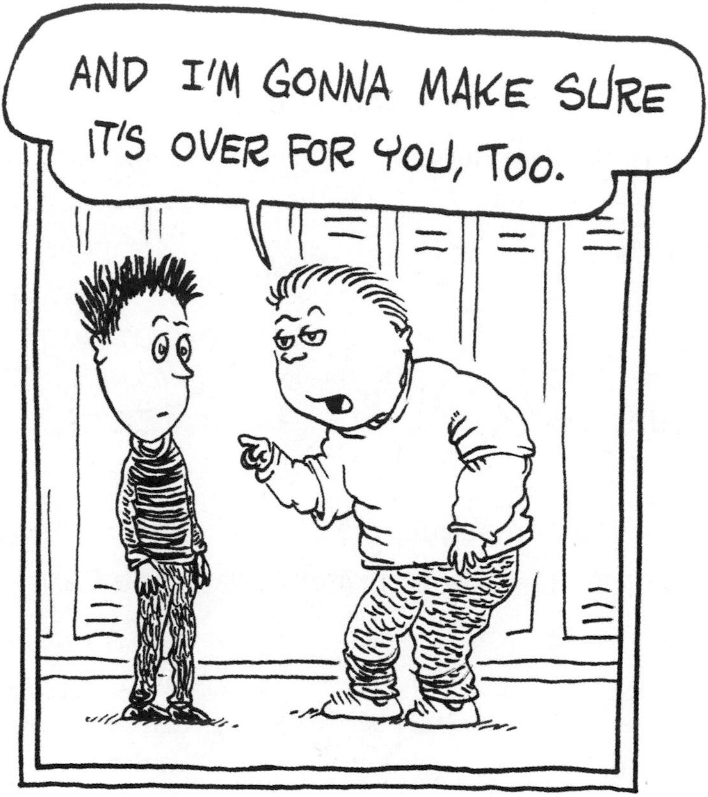
AND I'M GONNA MAKE SURE IT'S OVER FOR YOU, TOO.

# 8 IS THE SCARING OVER?

I'm sitting in my L.R.C. cubby turning those words over and over in my head.

Can they even do that? Take away the scaring? That's like taking away the air that I breathe!

OK, get a hold of yourself, Desmond. You can figure this out. Start with a list. What do we know?

So I pull a sheet out of my official spiral notebook of Super Scary Monster Effects and Gross Ideas, and start to write:

The End of Scares as we know it?

1) Principal Badonkus is replaced by Principal Needles →
There's a new sheriff in town!
Mrs. B
↳ Hates monsters and scares

2) Keith Schimsky is Needles's enforcer to make sure I don't scare.
Don't even think about it, Pucket!
New Ghost Buster

3) Carnival of Horrors is totally canceled. → OCTOBER

4) The Mountain Full of Monsters really is gone forever.

And then I notice something. See it, at the bottom there, right by the word "monsters"?

Yep, a tear splat.

I'm crying.

And the worst thing is, I'm crying in school. I'd rather eat a giant can of the cafetorium mixed vegetables than get caught crying in school. Thank goodness I'm in the study cubby. A good place for napping and, as it turns out, some private boy-weeping. I guess it was the last line that got me . . .

4) The Mountain Full of Monsters really is gone forever.

It never really hit me until just now. In the back of my head, I always figured my monsters would get a second chance in some horror attraction. And the Carnival of Horrors was it! Now I guess they won't.

Whoa, dude! You promised!

Weepy Weepums

Sorry! I didn't see it coming!

Oh, sure, the monsters will always have a place at my house as Halloween decorations, but it's not the same audience like a school-event audience. Besides, at Halloween, most people avoid my house like the plague.

So I'm sitting in my cubby trying to keep my sniffling to a minimum when—

I unfold the crumpled up ball of paper . . .

And I flip it over . . .

Oh, great. Now I'm laughing *and* crying. Thanks, Ricky.

I wipe my eyes and look behind me to see Ricky's face and so he can see me laughing at his comic.

Ooooo, was not expecting the librarian, Ms. Ruebbles. And Ricky's right behind her, holding his breath, trying not to bust out laughing.

And then, looking up at her, I can feel my face start to shift and I'm panicking. Hot tears fill my eyes and I quickly turn away. I always really liked Ms. Ruebbles because she's smart and funny and wears rubber band bracelets and knows almost as much about monsters as I do (all that reading!). But in that one moment that I looked up, she reminded me of my mom.

I feel her kneel down next to me.

"Yeah," I manage to sputter. "Just getting a cold, I guess."

Now maybe she'll go away. But I can feel that she's still there. Can't she tell I don't want to talk?

"Desmond," she starts slowly. "I know that life can be really hard, especially for seventh graders. So many impossible questions! So many questions it makes you crazy sometimes, right?"

"I guess," I say, slowly turning toward her.

"Answers," she says, as she dips down to eye level with me again. "Answers to all the world's questions. They're right here! But they aren't in neat piles. You have to dig for them; piece them together. And sometimes the answer is just a nice distraction from the things that worry you."

Maybe Ms. Ruebbles is right. She is pretty smart. One way to find out.

# 9 IN SEARCH OF...

Looking for the answer can be really tricky. Especially when you have as many questions as I do. I just think it was Ms. Ruebbles's way to get me to explore the L.R.C. and find stuff I never knew existed.

"Nobody would know what I was talking about! Not that they do now. Ain't that a kick in the head? OK, so maybe I ain't cooking with gas. Don't snap your cap, Sam!"

Nah, maybe not.

But Ms. Ruebbles wasn't kidding. This place is loaded with stuff: filmstrips, 16 mm movies and projectors, microfilm, old newspapers and audio tapes, CDs, DVDs, Blu-rays, vinyl records and record players—

And, of course, the books! It's like I'm seeing them for the first time. I didn't even know we had graphic novels! Tons of them! One cooler than the next! Some are even drawn by girls. (What?! I know!)

And there are so many how-to books: how to make birdhouses and scrapbooks and robots and cigar box banjos and clubhouse curtains and on and on . . .

There are also these other kinds of how-to books at the library, but I'm staying away from them.

So it is in this sea of films and records and magazines and books that I find myself, searching for the answer . . . and the question.

"Pssst! Hey. Creepy library kid. Read me!"

I've been here too long. The books are talking to me. I reach up and pull a book out, looking into the dark slot.

Pfft. It's Ricky, on the other side of the bookcase.

"How's it going?" he asks. "Did you find the thing yet?"

I DON'T EVEN *KNOW* WHAT I'M LOOKING FOR. SOME IDEA, I GUESS.

"An idea for what?"

"I don't know. Oh, but I found this while I was looking and I thought of you . . ."

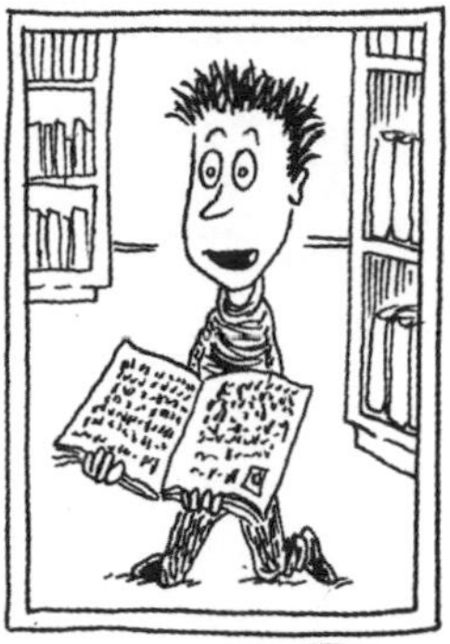

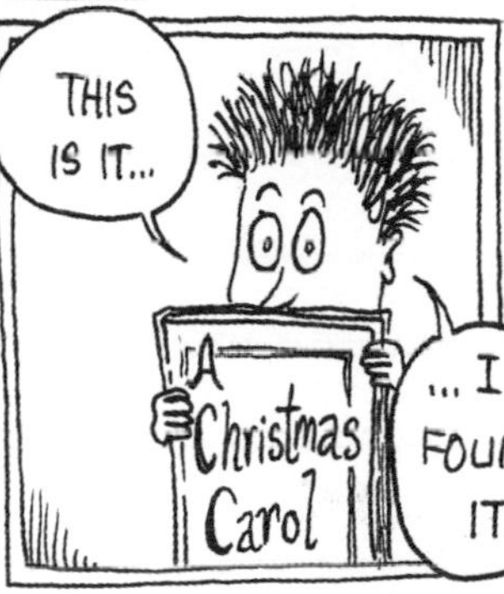
THIS IS IT...
A Christmas Carol
... I FOUND IT.

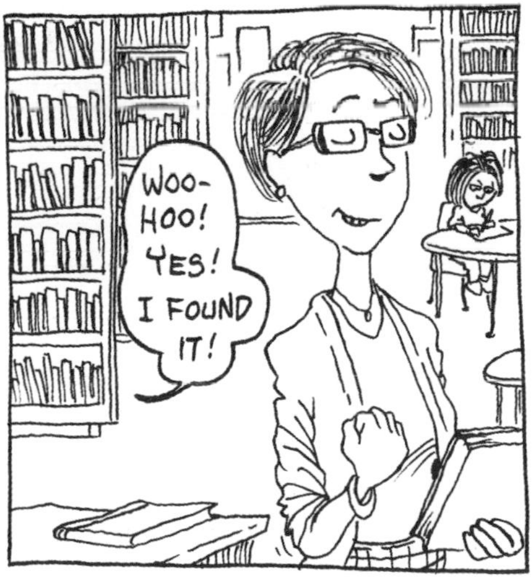
WOO-HOO! YES! I FOUND IT!

"With the ghosts of Christmas past and stuff? Isn't that a Muppet movie?"

"Listen, Ricky!" I say excitedly. "We've got to get our Scaring Company together after school! Special meeting, at my house."

"What for?"

# 10 GHOST WITH THE MOST

The room is pitch-black and we move slowly, following the noise of the deep, loud snoring.

I have only one set of night vision goggles, so I have to lead Becky through the maze of darkness. I'm pretty scared, but I have to admit it's nice having Becky with me. She makes me feel braver, even though she can't see two inches in front of her.

"Desmond, I can't—"

"Shhhh! No talking unless totally necessary! Only short whispers! And no using names, for sure!"

"Hey, *kid*," whispers Becky, and I can tell she's rolling her eyes in the darkness. "How about letting me take a turn with those night vision goggles?"

We're right outside the bedroom door, a good place to assemble our monster magic. I'm careful not to let the bag full of stuff clink and clank too much, but I don't think anything can be heard over that roar of snoring. If somebody can sleep through that, I'm pretty sure we could shoot off fireworks.

OK, I'm almost all set and Becky is ready with her extension cords and remote box. Now to check in with Ricky outside . . .

"We're moving into position now, Whoopee Boy 1. Ready the whitewash and wait for my cue."

"OK, Boss Fang, standing by and ready to rock!"

Becky hands me back the night vision goggles and we begin crawling.

I pull the strap on my creature cargo and it opens like small tent. Becky and I slip under the white folds. I click on a small red work light on the front of the goggles and look at Becky.

Becky hits the remote and the smoke machine starts belching out thick streams of fog. The snores stop and we hear a slight stirring in the bed in front of us.

"Cue whitewash," I whisper into my mic, and outside the bedroom window Ricky springs to action.

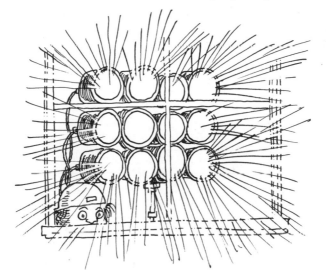

The room is bathed in harsh white light and the fog creeps across the floor and fills every corner.

I switch my mic setting to "broadcast voice distort," and launch into it . . .

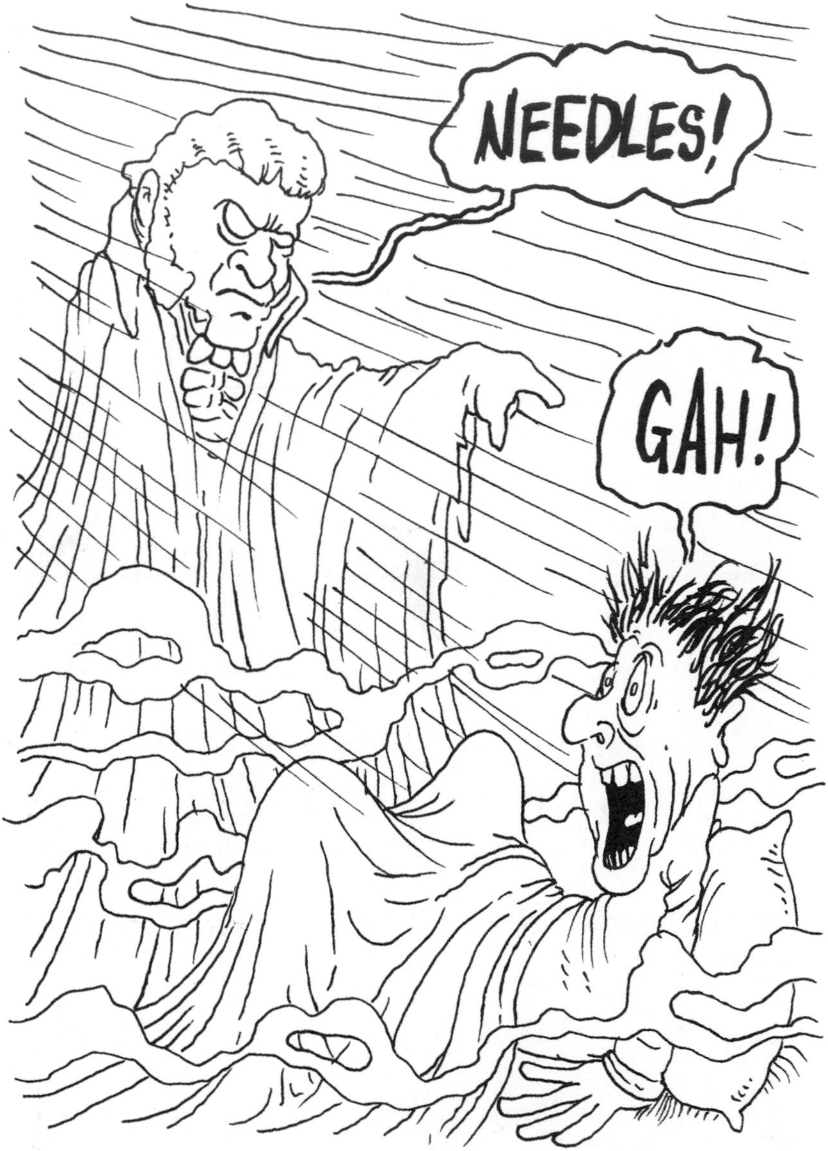
NEEDLES!
GAH!

"Wait! Wha—?" screams Mr. Needles. "Who are you?!"

"You don't recognize me?" I say in my best seriously spooky spirit voice.

"Not without my glasses!"

"OK," I sigh in the spirit voice. "Get them. I'll wait. Sheesh."

Mr. Needles fumbles at his night table, knocking over cups and books and bottles. I sigh. And then . . .

"**Was!** Now I am the **ghost** of J.J. Cloverfield, and YOU, Principal Needles, must answer for your deeds!"

"What do you want from me?" asks Mr. Needles.

# 11 THE NEXT DAY

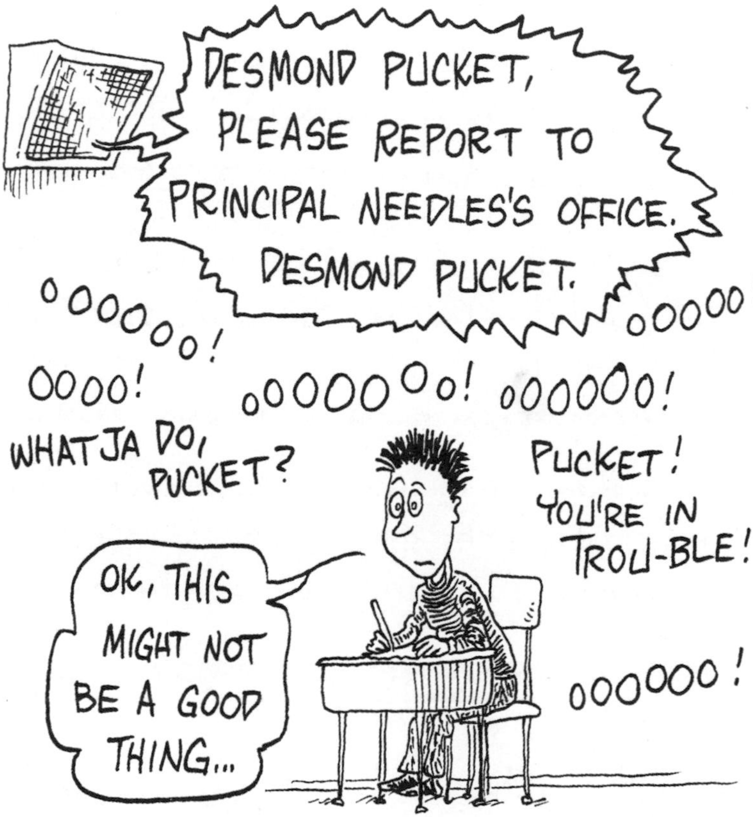
DESMOND PUCKET, PLEASE REPORT TO PRINCIPAL NEEDLES'S OFFICE. DESMOND PUCKET.
OOOOOOO!
OOOOO!
OOOO!
OOOOOOO!
OOOOOO!
WHATJA DO, PUCKET?
PUCKET! YOU'RE IN TROU-BLE!
OK, THIS MIGHT NOT BE A GOOD THING...
OOOOOO!

I slowly get up and head to the door as Mr. Oblio quiets down the classroom's cheers of doom. As I pass her desk, I look at Becky.

Sheesh, if I look *that* guilty standing in front of Needles, he's the iceberg and I'm the *Titanic*!

I start the long walk to the principal's office, taking my time so I can figure out a defense.

I don't see how Needles would know it was us last night. I'm pretty sure we made a clean getaway when he had the blankets pulled over his head!

I take the really long route to his office, but there's no avoiding it forever, and eventually I arrive. No line at his office this time. Dang. So I knock.

"Come in, Pucket."

"You are here, Mr. Pucket, because . . ."
Then Mr. Needles spins around to face me.

Then I notice something is very different about Mr. Needles: it's not just that he's unshaven or that he's wearing his suit jacket over his pajama shirt. No, it's that he's . . . he's . . . he's SMILING!

"Last night I had an epiphany! A visitation! *A great voice from beyond told me*—well, it doesn't matter . . . I feel like Ebenezer Scrooge on Christmas Day . . . ho ho ho!"

Holy crud! That ghost-from-the-past stuff really works! I'm not sure if people even know this, but that Charles Dickens guy was a *genius*!

Then me and Mr. Needles and J.J. Cloverfield dance around the dingy office, when out of nowhere . . .

"Principal Needles is going to let us put on the Carnival of Horrors after all! Woo hoo!"

"Yeah, I heard," says Keith. "We've got a lot of work to do."

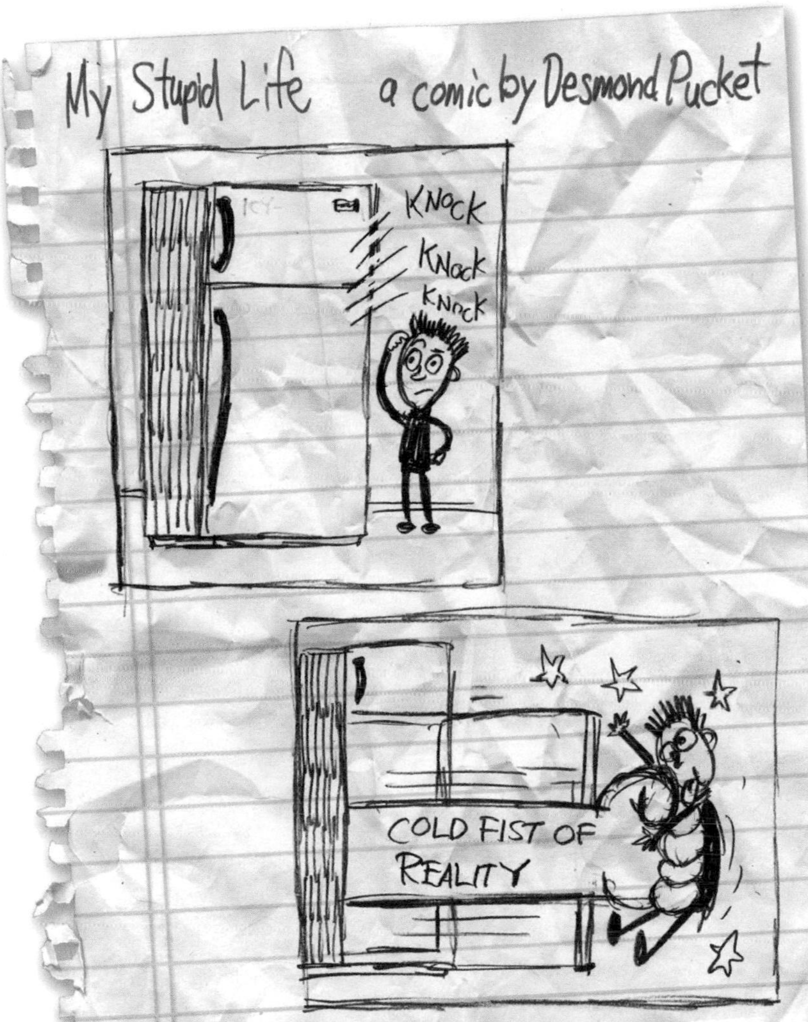
My Stupid Life a comic by Desmond Pucket
ICY
KNOCK
KNOCK
KNOCK
COLD FIST OF REALITY

# 12 THE FRIGHT FELLOWS

"I don't get it, Desmond," says Becky. "Why didn't you just tell Mr. Needles that you want to be in charge of the Haunted Cafetorium?"

HE WAS IN SUCH A GOOD MOOD, I WAS AFRAID OF JINXING IT!

"Besides, I'm just glad we have the whole Carnival of Horrors back. The ghost of Cloverfield really did the job and Mr. Needles is totally changed! I don't want to rock that boat! I'm afraid he might slip back to 'old Needles' at any second."

82

So now we're going to the cafetorium to meet with Keith and start planning the haunted house. The real trick is going to be keeping Keith under control.

When we get there, we see that Keith has already started building the thing . . . without us!

"Hey, Keith," I say. "What's going on? I thought maybe we'd do this thing together?"

"Sheesh, don't be such a jerk, Keith," says a voice from behind the black paper. "He just wants to help! Remember when he let *you* help!"

"Mom says you have to do what I say!" yells Keith. "I'm in charge!"

"Power hungry much?" Tina mutters, ducking back behind the paper. "I'm not on your weird team."

"Wait, who is on your team?" I ask.

"Yes, I have monster makers," says Keith. "Meet *the Fright Fellows*!"

"Really, dude?" I say to Keith. "This is your team of expert haunted house makers?"

"They're really good at nailing and gluing stuff."

"And I get out of Saturday detentions for this," shouts Mike.

"Isn't Little Jaimie supposed to be in high school?" I ask.

"Look, as long as they can follow directions," says Keith. "I've already got the whole thing planned out!"

"You do? Can I look at the plans?"

And then I see that Keith is clutching a spiral idea notebook a lot like mine. He hands me some torn-out sheets.

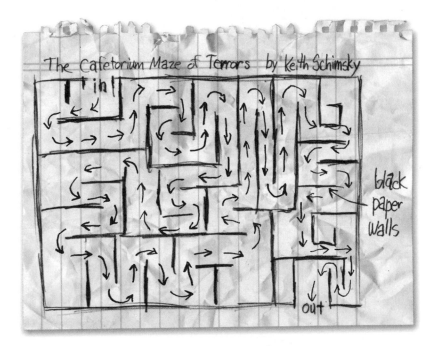

And page two . . .

"Wait, is that it? Just the maze and some glow-in-the-dark pictures that are supposed to be scary?"

"Yes, that's it," Keith snaps and grabs the pages from me.

"The last time you and I planned a scare together, I ended up in military school! No thanks!"

"What are you talking about, Keith?! That was your fault! If you did what I said—"

"Look, Desmond, Principal Needles said to keep you from scaring and I'm doing it because he got me out of that military camp . . ."

"But it's Mr. Needles's idea to bring the whole Carnival of Horrors back," I shout.

YEAH, I KNOW. HE CHANGED HIS MIND. AND I'M PRETTY SURE YOU HAD SOMETHING TO DO WITH THAT...

...BUT I'M STILL KEEPING MY WORD TO HIM, SO BACK OFF...

...THE HAUNTED CAFETORIUM IS MINE!

"So, what? That's it, Keith? You're totally cutting us out?"

"No, not all! We need lots of help hanging the black paper and painting the neon monsters!"

# 13 NOW WHAT?

It's only been a couple weeks, but I'm already totally lost in French. Great. Now I'm confused in two languages.

Conjugating verbs? That doesn't even sound legal. Why can't we just leave those poor verbs alone? Maybe that's why they make us change our first name for French class. We're all hiding from the verb police for unlawful conjugation.

Shee-zoo, I'm really starting to lose it. I shuffle through the piles of paper on my desk and then . . .

Hoo boy. As if I weren't already depressed enough about conjugating French verbs, I had to find this?

"Hey, Mister, what's doing?" my dad suddenly interrupts from behind. "Studies on a Friday night?!"

"You seem distracted, Desmond," the town's most well-respected dentist says using his oral-hygiene-tips voice. "Is there something on your mind, son?"

I carefully tuck the Haunted Cafetorium plans out of sight. Dad means well, but he's not a big supporter of my monster-y aspirations. The last thing he probably wants to hear is how bummed I am about getting knocked out of the Carnival of Horrors.

"Mom says there's a seventh grade dance at the school tonight," he continues. "Isn't there some nice young lady you'd like to take to that?"

"Eh, I really don't feel much like a dance, Dad."

"I think I just hit the nail on the head," Dad says triumphantly as he kneels down, bringing his head even with mine. "Trouble with the ladies?"

My dad might be a well-respected dentist and really know his molars from his bicuspids, and if I have a question about mouthwash or dental floss, he's my go-to guy. But when it comes to his ideas about "the ladies" . . . well . . . his advice is usually less than butt.

Actual scene from recent Dad "girl advice":

"ladies man," not so much.

important mustache movement

important pants

Desmond, my boy, Someday you'll understand about women that there's no understanding women.

Uh, yeah. Can I borrow your dental wax to make some new fangs?

Me, confused but polite

And since I get the feeling that he's about to give me the kind of useful information like you see above, I spring out of my chair and I grab my jacket.

"You know what, Dad? I think I might go to that dance. Maybe I'll stop by Ricky's and see what he wants to do."

It's getting cold out. The change of seasons. It's even starting to smell like Halloween. But that just makes me think of the Carnival of Horrors, which makes me feel more depressed.

Ricky's is about a block away but I take the shortcut through the Seltzers' hedges, the same way to school. I find that I'm running without even knowing it, and the rhythm of my feet is pounding,

"Figure it out, figure it out, figure it out." I have to find a way into the Carnival of Horrors or I'm going to go crazy.

I head in the direction of Ricky's, but I have one stop first: the shed is the only thing that will clear my head. I dig the hidden key out of the small broken Santa flowerpot on the ground by the door and . . .

"I have to thank your grandparents again for letting me keep the monsters here."

"Aw, they don't care. This shed used to be stuffed with their Christmas junk. Now they keep the Christmas junk in the house year-round."

SO ARE WE DOING THIS SCHOOL DANCE, OR WHAT?

# 14 DANCIN' IN THE DARK

Every middle school dance has to have a theme. It's sort of an unwritten law. A middle school dance without a theme is like a clown with no makeup. In fact, it's exactly like a clown with no makeup. Did you ever see a seventh grade boy dance? Very clownish. And I am *Exhibit A . . .*

So please, always let us have a theme. It gives us something to hide behind. Just no clown themes.

This year's first official seventh grade dance theme is . . . *Dancin' in the Dark!* The best theme ever! Seventh grade boy dancing is especially good when no one can see it.

The entire gym is lit by black lights, which makes us all glow in different colors. And we're all given different kinds of glow-in-the-dark stuff:

Ricky and I smear on some face paint and wrap some glo tape around our arms and legs. I try to keep it simple, but Ricky goes a little nuts with the colored tape.

We mix into the crowd of kids and look around to see who's here. And then, *she* appears as if by magic . . . a Day-Glo vision of neon fabulocity!

Everything she's wearing is perfect for the black lights. Even her lips and eye shadow are glowing! And her hair! She looks like an alien queen who just stepped out of a nuclear waste dump!

Donna Lambert. I should've know. She doesn't miss anything. You really have to be careful what you say and do around Donna Lambert. She's the eyes and ears of Cloverfield Junior High! And the big mouth:

That's her gossip column in our school newspaper. She doesn't use any last names, but everybody always knows who she's talking about. She mostly reports on who's-making-out-with-who or who's-cheating-on-who or who's-breaking-up-with-who.

Donna Lambert does, however, report who's-crushing-on-who and that's something I really don't want everybody to see in print. So I quickly distract her with the worst thing I can think of . . .

A slow dance. I turn to look at the crowd. I spot Ricky dancing with Katie Fine.

But where's Tina? I start to move around the shuffling pack of kids when . . .

That can't be Becky! Becky hates dances! Becky makes fun of the school dances! And she's wearing a dress? But the most important thing—

"They're the hot story of the night! That's Bryan Skillman, center on our soccer team. A real star! Those two came here together!"

"Or do I smell a *love triangle*?!"

"Actually, no, that was me, sorry," says Ricky, who snuck up behind us. "The chicken 'n' waffle corn chips at the snack bar made my belly go every which-y-way."

"You're disgusting, DiMarco," Donna says with a curl of her upper lip that looks like she means it.

And then I notice: the slow music has stopped and the fast music is cranked and pounding again.

The old gym, in case you're wondering, is just that: the old gym. The old gym is old and musty and falling apart, so instead of fixing it up, they built a new gym.

I guess they figured they'd always do something with the old gym, only they never did. So they just keep it locked up. But every kid knows how to get in. And every kid knows about the perfect make out spot at the very top of the old bleachers.

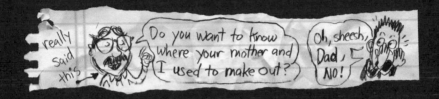

Well, I don't really know anybody who's actually been up in those old bleachers, but that's how the story goes.

I pull off all of the glowing tape, paint, and plastic bits and head in the direction of the old gym.

# 15 THE OLD GYM

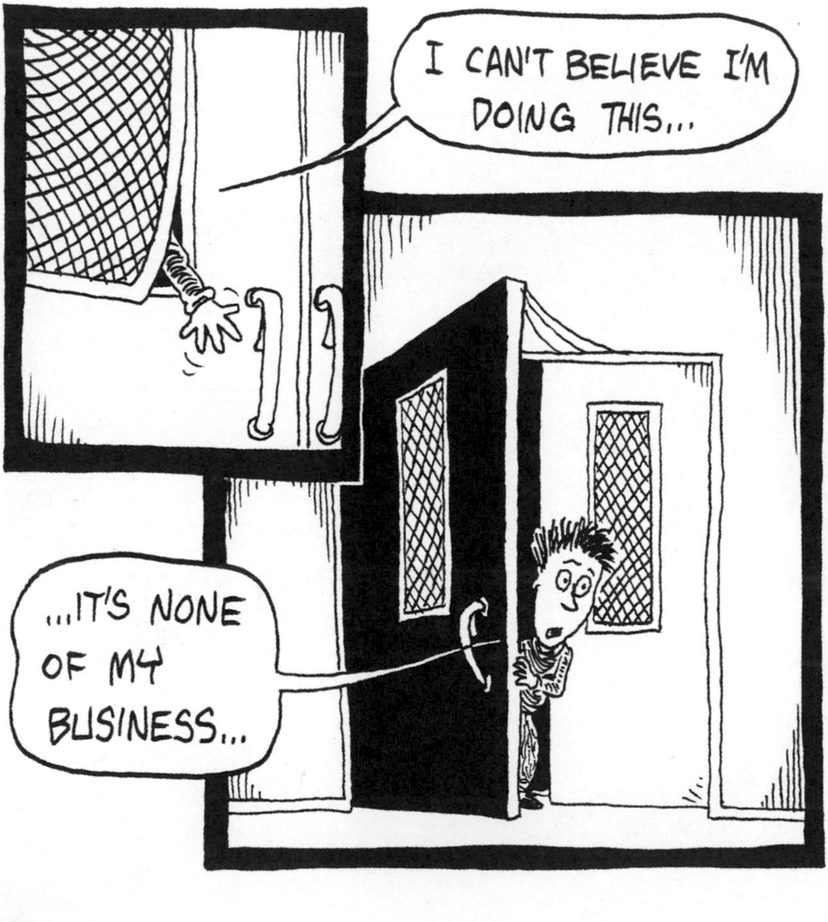
I CAN'T BELIEVE I'M DOING THIS...
...IT'S NONE OF MY BUSINESS...

"If Becky wants to come to the old gym with Bryan Skillman, like Donna said, what do I care?"

It's total darkness in the old gym, except for a small spill of light coming from some windows near the ceiling. I reach into my pocket, ready to put an end to the black space in front of me.

I . . . I can't do it. I put the flashlight away and start quietly backing up toward the old gym door.

"Ow, holy turds, Desmond!" shouts Ricky. "For such little feet, you sure know how to crush a toe!"

"Shhhhhhhhh!" I whisper as I cover Ricky's mouth.

"Why are you shushing me?" Ricky says through my fingers.

"Because I think Becky is up there in the top bleachers!"

"She's at the snack bar with Bryan—*OMG*, Desmond! That's why you're in here? You thought she was in the make out spot with Bryan?! You were spying on Becky?!"

"No, not spying! I was just curious, is all—"

"Yeah, well, you might be too late," Ricky says. "Seems like she's really into that Skillman kid."

"Good for him. I don't care anyway."

"Riiiiiiiight. So did you see it?"

"See what?"

"The spot at the top of the bleachers! I want to see it!"

"I never turned my flashlight on."

"Did you try the light switch?" Ricky says as he gropes along the wall in the dark. "Got it!"

Only three of the lights actually work, so the whole gym has a sort of creepy brown glow. There's dust and dirt everywhere, and more spiderwebs than the Mountain Full of Monsters ever thought of having.

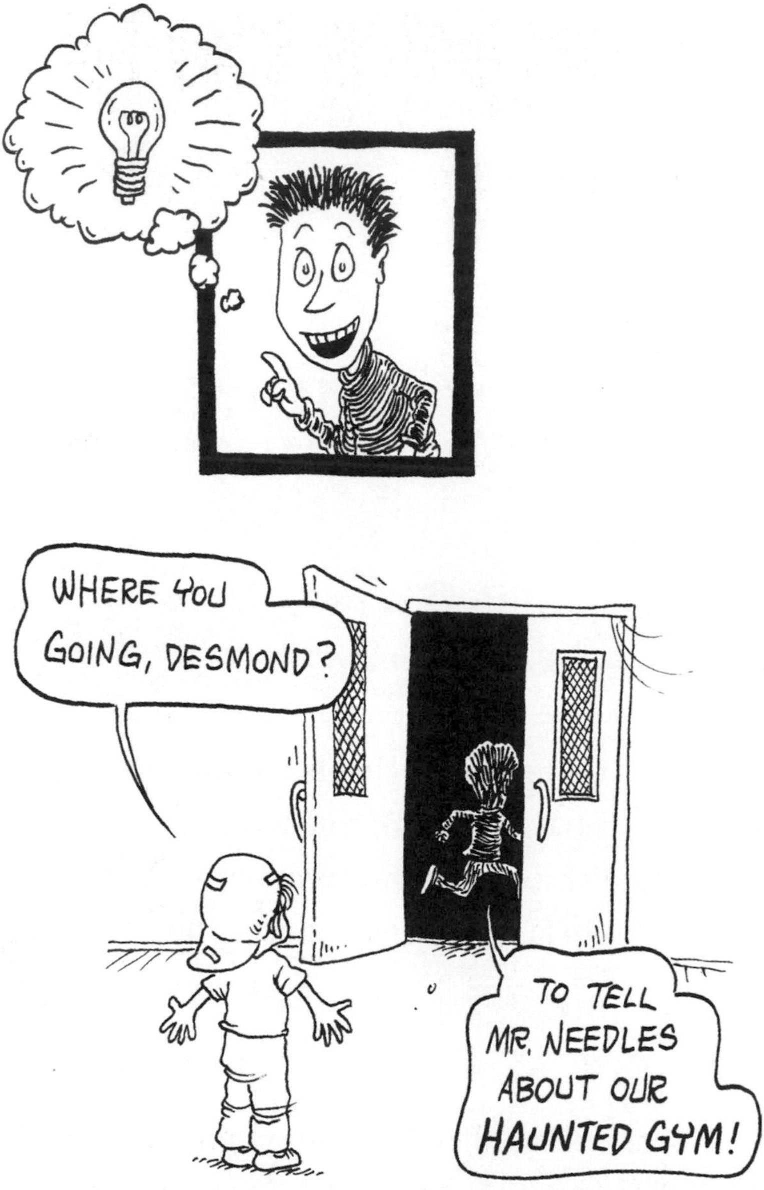
WHERE YOU GOING, DESMOND?
TO TELL MR. NEEDLES ABOUT OUR HAUNTED GYM!

# 16 PLAN 9 FROM OUTER SPACE

That's the name of this weird science fiction movie made in 1959 by director Ed Wood. The movie is so bad that it's good.

"Unspeakable Horrors from outer space paralyze the living and resurrect the dead!"

Actual movie poster looks like this! I swear, I have it in my room!

That's also what I'm calling my plan for the old gym. Plan 9 from Outer Space. Because it's so bad that it's good.

But before I can pitch my idea to Mr. Needles, I have to figure a couple things out. And since I'm still at school for the dance, I head to the L.R.C. Where the answers are!

I slip inside and bolt over to the architecture and building section, because I remember seeing this one book—

I lay the book out and start sweeping through the pages, looking for the old blueprints of Cloverfield Junior High. It was built back in the 1950s I think, so—

I pull out some scraps of paper and start writing notes. The ideas are really coming now, but I still have a problem . . .

And that's when I hear something.

"Sniff . . . sniff . . . sniff."

We are not alone, folks. And I don't mean aliens. I mean that someone else is in the L.R.C.!

"Sniff . . . sniff."

"I didn't know you . . . what are you doing in here?! Students aren't allowed in the L.R.C. after school hours!"

"Oh, I'm sorry! The door was unlocked so I—"

"sniff . . . sniff."

"Are you OK, Ms. Ruebbles?"

Libraries are great for studying, but I guess they're also the perfect place for a good cry.

"Well, Desmond, I guess you'll find out soon enough . . ."

"Oh, believe me, it's not because I want to," Ms. Ruebbles continues. "It's because they cut my job to two days a week and I can't afford to work for just two days. So I have to find another job."

"But . . . who's going to be librarian?"

"Oh, they'll find somebody. And use parent volunteers for the other three days."

"Yeah, it's just so expensive for me, Desmond, with two kids in day care . . . well, it's complicated."

"I'm sorry, Ms. Ruebbles. I wish I could help."

"Aw, I know you do, Desmond . . ."

"Ms. Ruebbles, remember how you told me that the answers are in the library?"

"Yes."

"Well, maybe sometimes the answers aren't all in the books . . ."

# 17 THE PITCH

"Though I confess," says Mr. Needles, "I could have done without the fart piano music."

"Oh, that was just a little fun to break up all the talk, talk, talk," says Ricky. "My idea."

"Yes, I guessed that much," Mr. Needles says, then turns to me. "Mr. Pucket, the Carnival of Horrors already has a Haunted Cafetorium . . . why do we need a Haunted Gym?"

BECAUSE WE CAN RAISE **TWICE** AS MUCH MONEY, AND **SAVE** LIBRARIAN RUEBBLES'S JOB!

"But the old gym is a mess!"

"Yeah, I know," I say. "But Becky's father, Janitor DeWicky, works here, and he also does construction. He and some of his friends volunteered to clean it up and make sure it's safe!"

BECKY WAS SUPPOSED TO BE HERE TO TELL YOU, BUT I GUESS SHE FORGOT.

That's kind of weird. We practiced this all week! How could Becky forget? Where is she?

"But *two* haunted rides?" asks Mr. Needles. "How do we know people will want to go in *both*? I know I can barely stand one!"

"Here's the fun part: we make it a *competition*!"

"And then, at the end of the carnival, we'll count the votes and crown the King of All Scare Rides!"

"And I've got another idea," says Keith from his usual spot next to Mr. Needles's desk. "Let's make it even *more* interesting . . ."

"Aw, c'mon, let's be real here," I say. "I mean, if Disney gives me millions to make a new haunted house in the Magic Kingdom, I'm not going to say 'no'!"

"All right, school life then. The loser gives up scaring for the rest of junior high and high school!"

"Just one moment, gentlemen," Mr. Needles sternly interrupts from the depths of his chair. "I don't *like* this whole idea of two competing haunted houses!"

I really like this new Needles! But I'm always afraid that at any second, the clock is going to strike midnight and he's going to turn back into a pumpkin! A moldy, mean pumpkin.

"Yes, yes, boys, very excited now, don't dillydally," Mr. Needles says, clapping his hands and patting the sculpture on his desk. "All for the good of the school! I'm sure Mr. Cloverfield would approve!"

"Aw, man, Ricky! This is insane! I can't believe that Mr. Needles went for it! We have to tell Becky so that we—"

But Ricky isn't listening to me. He's standing by Jessie O'Neil, who is handing out school newspapers.

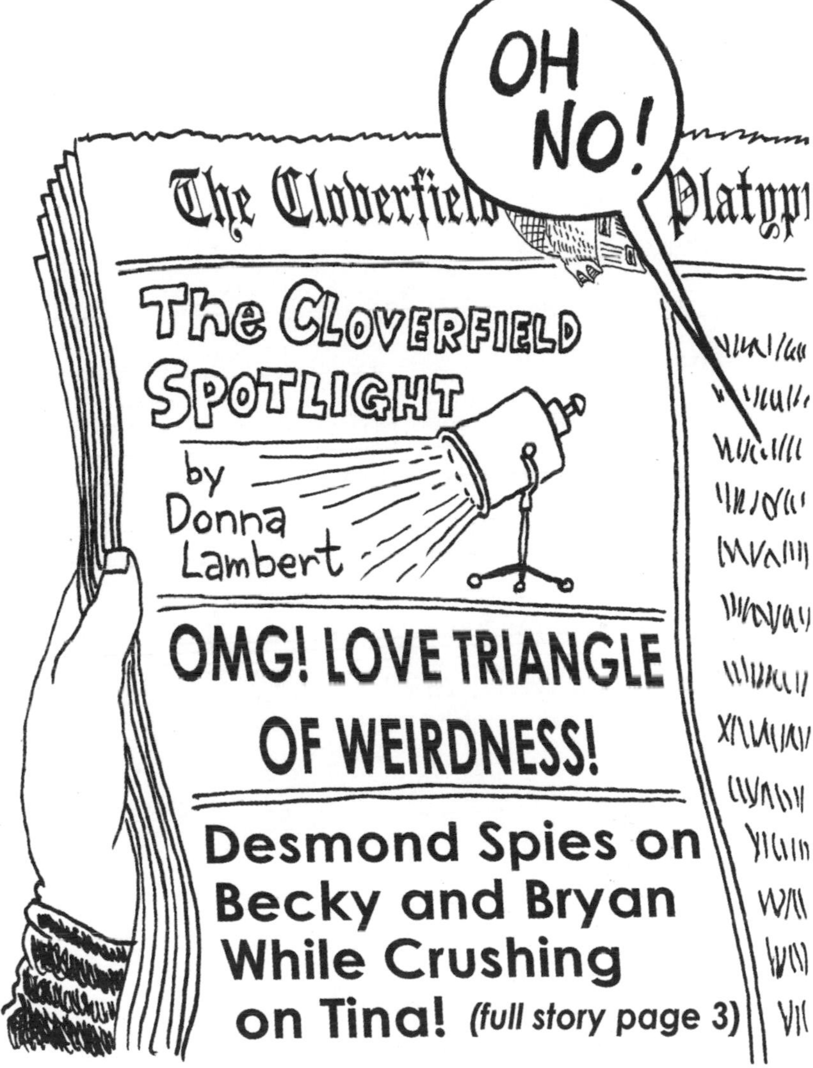
OH NO!
The Cloverfield Platypu
The Cloverfield Spotlight
by Donna Lambert
OMG! LOVE TRIANGLE OF WEIRDNESS!
Desmond Spies on Becky and Bryan While Crushing on Tina! (full story page 3)

# 18 LOVE STINKS

"There's nothing in this story about me and Katie Fine! Didn't Donna see us slow dancing together?! That's bigger news than your lame four-person love triangle, which technically is a love *square*—"

"Shut up, Ricky! I have to figure this thing out!"

Take a breath, Pucket. Maybe it's not so bad. I turn to the page of Donna's article.

**SPOTLIGHT**
by Donna Lambert

(continued from front page)
And who did I spot following Becky and Bryan into the Old Gym? None other than our very own Demon Desmond! Was he trying to spy on the love birds even though I just caught him at the dance crushing on Miss Tina? Watch this space for further weirdness, dear readers!
Dance in the Dark was a hit with

OK, this is beyond horrible. This is chomping-a-piece-of-candy-thinking-it's-blueberry-flavored-and-discovering-it's-a-mentholated-cough-drop horrible! This is stale-cheese-curl cray cray!

All right, no biggie, so the whole school thinks I'm a creepy, spying, stalker-weirdo from outer space. That's nothing new, right? But Becky, she's too smart to believe this gossip junk. She'll listen to me when I explain to her what really happened, right?

I'm pretty sure that's Becky talking. It's hard to see with a face full of spoiled potato sludge.

"No, Becky, wait," I sputter as I wipe at my face with the newspaper. "You don't understand!"

"What don't I understand? That you followed me and Bryan and then tried to spy on us? What, were you jealous? I thought you were all about Tina! Do you like me now or something?"

"And until you get your head screwed on right, count me out!"

"Oh, boy, Pucket. It's not looking good, brother! Only three weeks until the Carnival of Horrors, when I'm crowned King of All Fright Rides . . . "

"Hah! Dream on, Keith! When I'm done with my Haunted Gym, your Haunted Cafetorium will wish it was never born!"

"Aw, man, Pucket!" laughs Keith as he walks away. "You're pathetic! I love to watch you squirm!"

But Keith's right. I'm sunk without Becky and her dad. I'll never be able to pull off the Haunted Gym with just me and Ricky!

"It's because of your stupid newspaper story that my life is totally in the toilet."

"Oooooo! Can I use that as my next headline? 'A Life Gone Totally Toilet'! I like it!"

"Donna! When does the next school paper come out?"

"Uh . . . in two weeks. But I—"

"Perfect! I have a great story for you! You're going to love it! It will make you school-famous! But you have to let me write the headline for the article!"

"I don't know, Pucket. You're sort of a mondo-dweeb. What makes you think I'm going to like your story idea?"

# 19 THE BECKY SITUATION

Time for some deep pondering and fast plan making. I grab my spiral notebook of Super Scary Monster Effects and Gross Ideas, four No. 2 Black Warrior pencils, and my lucky partially eaten pinkie eraser (don't ask me why Douglass Zulli bit it in half in fifth grade, but I've felt sorry for it ever since), and I unlock the Desmond think tank.

It's not long before Ricky joins me in the drafty shed with the really important supplies: cheddar jalapeño Cheetos and four bottles of Cheerwine soda.

"So what's the big deal, Desmond . . ."

... JUST TELL BECKY THAT YOU LIKE HER.

"Yeah, right! And then she tells me that's sweet and she really likes Bryan Skillman and let's just be friends. Guh. No thanks."

BESIDES, SHE AND EVERYBODY IN THE WHOLE SCHOOL THINKS I'M TOTALLY INTO TINA SCHIMSKY!

"I have to tell you, dude," Ricky says around a mouthful of Cheetos. "That's what I thought, too!"

"It's hard to explain," I say. "Me liking Tina is something that I always did since I started at Cloverfield Junior High. It's kind of magical! From the first time I ever saw her—"

OH, BROTHER! DID ANGELS FLY OUT OF THE SKY SINGING "TINA! TINA!" AND HAND OUT FREE MILKYWAY BARS?

SOMETHING LIKE THAT...

"Anyways, from then on it was something that was always there. It's this special feeling that makes me happy to hang on to . . ."

"You mean like a habit?"

"Yeah, I guess. But Becky's different. Becky's smart and funny and she always comes through in a pinch. A clutch player, you know. And that girl can make *anything* from a 9-volt battery and two wires!"

WHICH IS WHY I HAVE TO COME UP WITH A REALLY SPECIAL AND CREATIVE WAY TO TELL HER, "I'M SORRY."

"Maybe you just did," Ricky says.

"Huh?"

That's when Ricky pulls the mic from under his hat and puts it up to his mouth.

"OK, so wait. This is a setup?" I gasp. "You heard everyth—you were spying on me this whole time?!"

Oh, yeah, there's that Becky left hook I know. She must've forgiven me. She only gives a beat down like that to her closest friends.

"Aw, don't be mad, Desmond," Ricky says. "It was my idea! I can't have my friends fighting when we've got buckets of work to do on our Haunted Gym!"

"Actually, I felt a lot better after I pelted you with those rotten potatoes," Becky says. "But your 'I'm sorry' was still nice to hear."

"Could you speak up? Somebody hit me with a face full of mashed potatoes and I think there's still some stuck in my left ear."

WELL, C'MON, YOU GUYS! LET'S STOP FARTING AROUND AND GET OVER TO THE OLD GYM!

OH, WAIT... I HAVE TO LOCK UP THE SHED!

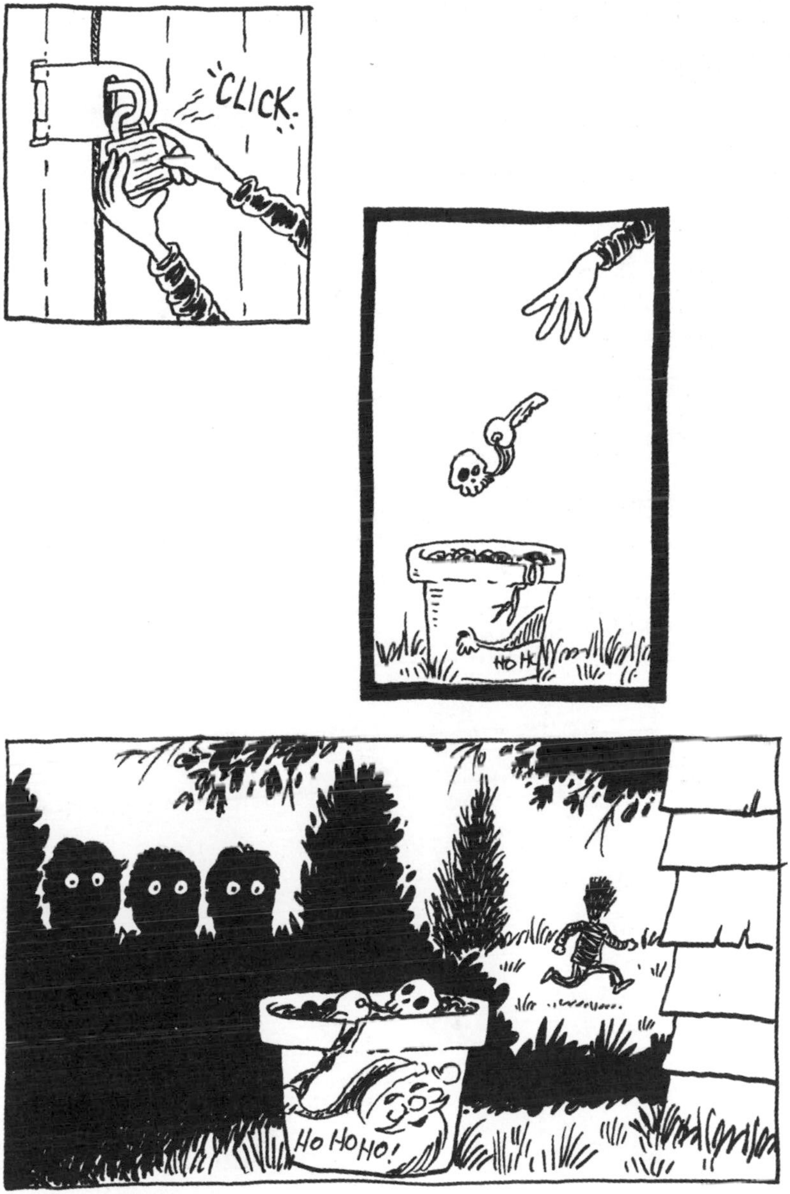
CLICK.
HO HO HO!

# 20 THE GHOSTIFICATION OF THE OLD GYM

The old gym was built in 1952, but then in 1984 they built the new gym and left the old gym just sitting there. This great big room frozen in time. Like the bell rang at the end of class one day and then nobody ever came back.

climbing rope

Though it smells like they forgot to take that stinky sock scent.

that horse thing

deflated basketball

There's junk and dust and dirt everywhere, but we break out the brooms and green plastic garbage bags, and pretty soon it looks kind of OK.

Seeing all of the old gym stuff helps the ghostification plans bake in my brain, and between the cleaning and fixing, I sketch in my spiral notebook of Super Scary Monster Effects and Gross Ideas.

Since I'm competing with Keith for the best haunted ride ever, I have to come up with some super crazy scares of complete awesomeness that stick to the theme of a haunted gym . . .

DESMOND PUCKET
"Gourmet of Gore"

HAUNTED GYM

TOP SECRET! →IDEAS!!!

① The Zombie Lockers!

Moving Zombies

Old lockers →

② The Hall of Sweaty Gym socks

Water squirts

And then I really start thinking: what if half of the ride is a walk-through . . .

. . . and the other half is a drive-through! A cool idea, but how can I pull that off? And then it hits me!

OK, I know you're probably thinking, "How're you going to get some big kids to wheel around a bunch of smaller kids in a wheelbarrow?" Good question. But that doesn't matter right now. The idea comes first. The "how" comes later. And just so you know, candy bribes usually work pretty well.

It takes a whole week of working after school and whenever Mr. DeWicky can come, but eventually the old gym is ready! Becky even rewired the broken lights and her dad fitted them with blue and green and red bulbs. Now the place glows with a sickly, scary color, like Stephen King's night-light.

"Let me get this straight," Mr. DeWicky says. "We spent all this time cleaning out the dead bugs and spiderwebs just so you can fill it back up with plastic bugs and fake spiderwebs? Makes complete sense!"

Kyle the bus kid is waiting outside of the old gym to drive us over to Ricky's grandparents' shed to pick up the monsters. Right now, Kyle and my sister Rachel are broken up, which is a good thing for me. I won't have to pay Rachel's usual boyfriend rental fee.

"Here we are, little bit," says Kyle as we pull up in front of Ricky's house.

"I told you a billion times to stop calling me that!" I shout, kicking Kyle's seat from behind.

OH, I'M SORRY, LITTLE BIT. I DIDN'T MEAN TO CALL YOU LITTLE BIT, LITTLE BIT. IT WON'T HAPPEN AGAIN, LITTLE BIT.

This from the kid who wears a belt buckle shaped like a bus. Sheesh.

Ricky, Becky, and I jump out of Kyle's van and head to the monster shed. I grab the key out of the cracked flowerpot.

OK, BOYS, YOU READY TO COME OUT AND PLAY?

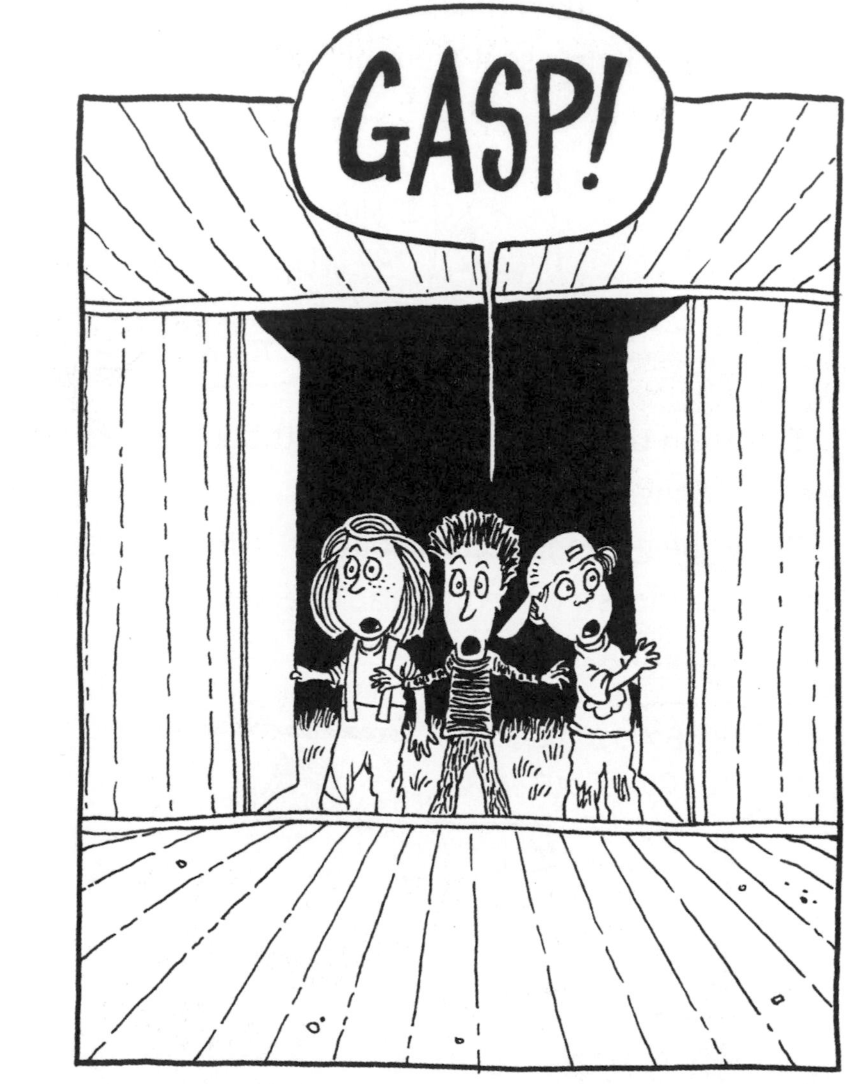
GASP!

# 21 MISSING MONSTERS

Now I know how all the Whos down in Whoville felt on Christmas morning after a visit from the Grinch. Though I'm pretty sure Ricky, Becky, and I won't be meeting in the village square to sing, "Fah Who for-aze, Dah Who dor-aze."

And we all immediately think the same thing:

"We should call the police!" Ricky says. "They'll find your monsters and maybe even throw Keith in jail!"

"Or we should at least tell Mr. Needles! He'll kick Keith back to military school!" finishes Becky.

"No!"

We all spin around. It's Tina Schimsky.

"Ha, so you admit he stole the monsters!" shouts Ricky. "And I don't think I'd call Keith 'little.'"

"Don't listen to her, Desmond," Becky whispers in my ear. "She's the enemy. She's on *their* team!"

"Not anymore," Tina says quickly. "I quit. I want to join you guys and help with your Haunted Gym."

"And I promise to get your monsters back!" Tina says, ignoring Ricky. "I'll figure out where Keith hid them and we'll steal them back!"

"You don't know where they are?" I ask.

"No, he won't say. But I swear I'll find out—"

"What happens if you don't?" interrupts Ricky.

I look at Becky and she gives me the usual eye-roll-and-sigh combo. She already knows how this is going . . .

"We can't call the cops and we can't tell Mr. Needles," I decide finally. "Keith will get in loads of trouble and they'll just shut down our rides or the whole Carnival of Horrors. Then we won't be able to help the library or Ms. Ruebbles."

"I swear we'll get your monsters back! Just leave it to me! You can trust me!"

"Yeah, that's what *I'm* worried about," says Ricky. "The Carnival of Horrors is going to be here and we're going to have the only haunted ride without any haunts!"

"What's the matter with you, Desmond?! Don't you even care that your monsters were stolen?!"

"Of course I care, Ricky! But I'm just thinking there might be a way to turn this missing monsters thing into our favor!"

"How?" says Becky, with a look that shows she isn't believing anything I say.

# 22 THE TRUST THING

"OK, I get it. You don't trust her," I say. "But don't you guys trust me?"

It's been five days since Tina told us she'd get our stolen monsters back from Keith, and from the look they're giving me across the art table, things aren't getting any better.

Becky, Ricky, and I are all in art class doing that most boring of all art projects: the coil pot.

It needs no sharp tools or messy glues. The instructions are simple. And since rolling clay into long tube shapes is mind-numbing, even the most disruptive kid falls into the "coil pot trance." This is the perfect art class project for the art teacher who needs to catch up on sleep.

"I mean, you have to admit that Tina's been working really hard helping us finish the Haunted Gym in time for the Carnival of Horrors," I say while rolling my clay tubes.

"So where are all the monsters she promised to find?" says Ricky, rolling his coil so long it starts to hang off the table.

"Yeah, Keith steals your precious monsters and totally gets away with it . . ."

...ALL BECAUSE THE BEAUTIFUL AND AMAZING TINA BEGGED FOR MERCY!

"Now Keith has all *our* monsters for his Haunted Cafetorium, and all we get is his prissy sister. I say we pay Keith back by sabotaging his attraction, too!"

"Hold it, no! You guys just have to trust me on this one! I've totally got a plan. You'll see!"

# KNOCK KNOCK KNOCK

"Huh? Whazzat?" Mr. Dreshler says through his nap stupor.

"It's the door, Mr. Dreshler. Can I get it?" asks Rusty Wheeler, already half out of his seat with hand stretched toward the knob. Rusty is always the first to open a door or window. It's sort of his thing. I guess everybody needs to be good at something.

"Uh, yeah, Rusty, get that," says Mr. Dreshler before slipping back into dreamland.

That's what I've been waiting for! As Rusty marches importantly toward the teacher's desk with the pile of papers, I grab a copy from the top.

I stare at the front page for a few seconds, and then:

# 23 THE CLUBFLUBBER STORY

"'Some weird things have been happening during the cleanup of the old gym,'" Becky says, reading aloud Donna Lambert's front page story, "'and I don't mean seeing Ricky pushing a broom.'"

Becky continues: "'While checking in with Demon Desmond and his monster magicians to see how next week's Carnival of Horrors Haunted Gym is coming together, this reporter was shocked and unbelieving to hear stories of how the old gym *really is haunted*.'"

me

OK, Hold the phone! So you want to know how I got this story in the Cloverfield Platypus? CHECK IT OUT!

So I get Donna Lambert to come to the Old Gym...

Hurry up, Pucket. I'm bored already!

and I tell her about all the strange things that have been happening...

The lights go on and off by themselves!

bad wires in gym.

161

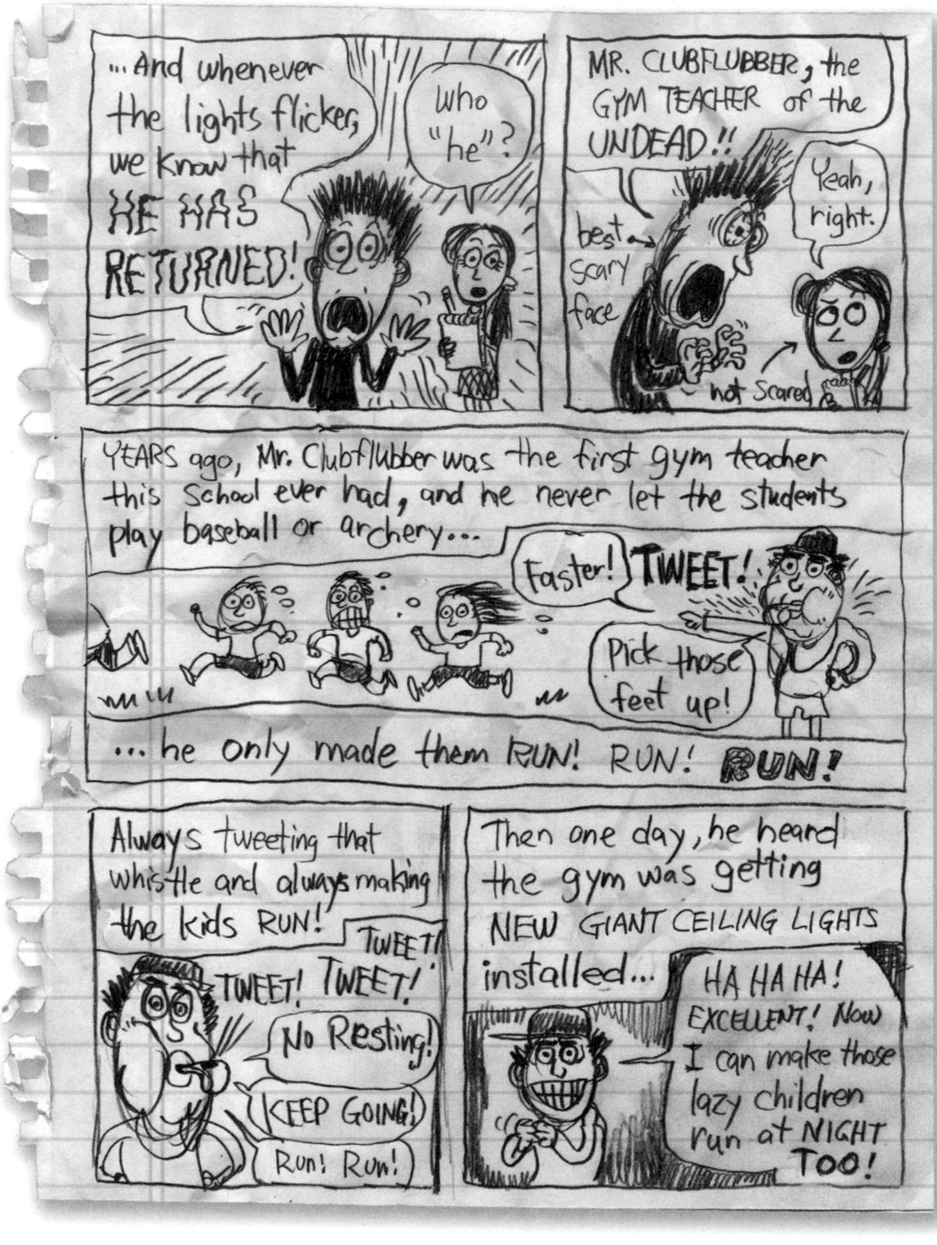
...And whenever the lights flicker, we know that HE HAS RETURNED!
Who "he"?
MR. CLUBFLUBBER, the GYM TEACHER of the UNDEAD!!
Yeah, right.
best scary face
not scared
YEARS ago, Mr. Clubflubber was the first gym teacher this school ever had, and he never let the students play baseball or archery...
Faster!
TWEET!
Pick those feet up!
...he only made them RUN! RUN! RUN!
Always tweeting that whistle and always making the kids RUN!
TWEET!
TWEET! TWEET!
No Resting!
KEEP GOING!
Run! Run!
Then one day, he heard the gym was getting NEW GIANT CEILING LIGHTS installed...
HA HA HA! EXCELLENT! Now I can make those lazy children run at NIGHT TOO!

But the electricians were taking too long, and the gym was closed while the work was in progress...

Dang! All the running that we're missing!

... So Mr. Clubflubber decided to finish the job himself!

Everyone is so lazy!

I'll have these gym lights working in no time!

Unfortunately for Mr. Clubflubber, electrician is not the job he's cut out for...

The next day, all they found was two sneakers and a pile of ashes.

Mr. Clubflubber

163

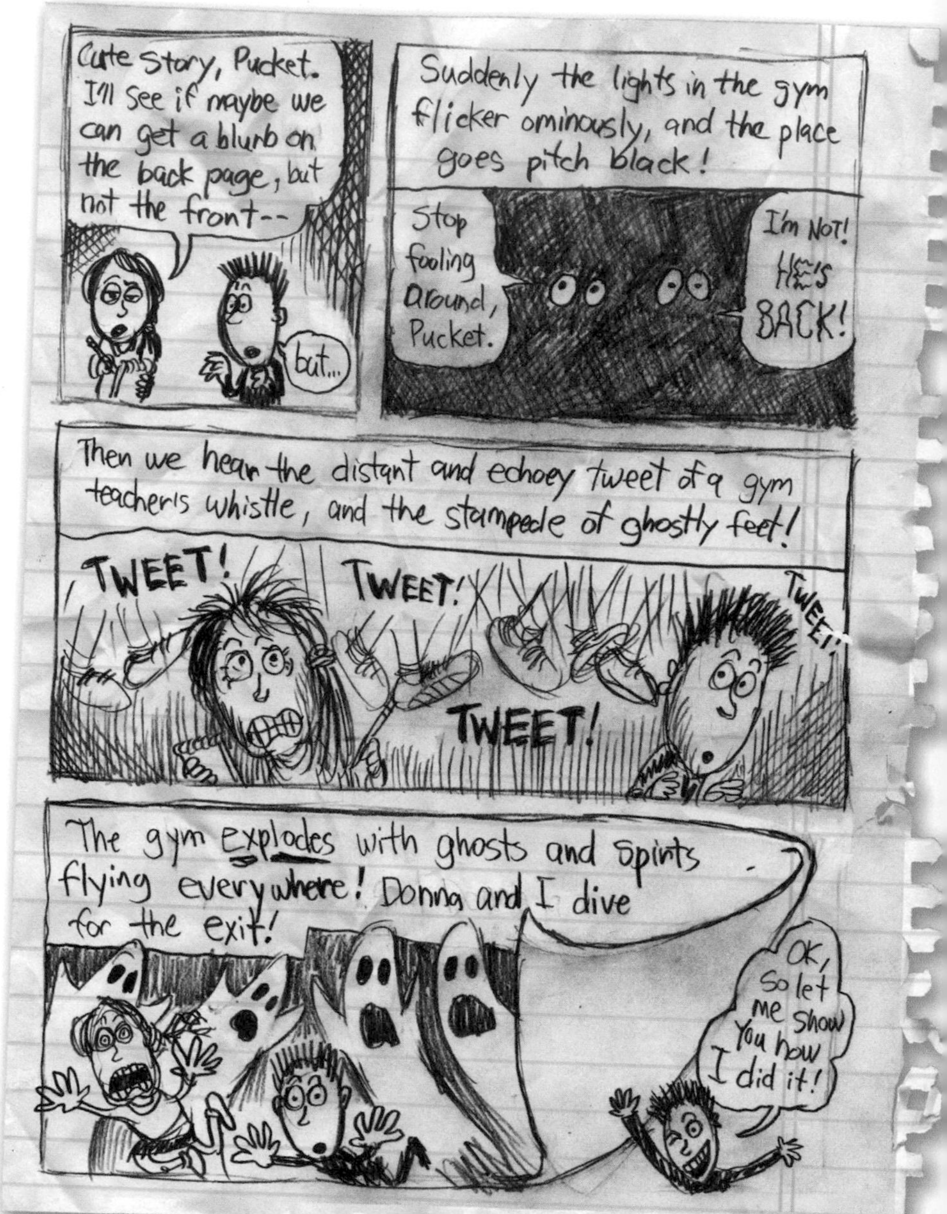
Cute Story, Pucket. I'll see if maybe we can get a blurb on the back page, but not the front--
but...
Suddenly the lights in the gym flicker ominously, and the place goes pitch black!
Stop fooling around, Pucket.
I'm NOT! HE'S BACK!
Then we hear the distant and echoey tweet of a gym teacher's whistle, and the stampede of ghostly feet!
TWEET!
TWEET!
TWEET!
TWEET!
The gym explodes with ghosts and spirits flying everywhere! Donna and I dive for the exit!
OK, So let me show you how I did it!

The easy part was the sound effects...

A remote ① control...

Ricky set this up

SCARY SOUNDZ

② Starts sounds on my laptop...

TWEET!

③ Which is attached to a big speaker!

The ghostly feet was a looping gif animation projected on a SCRIM (that's a gauzy piece of cloth.)

projector

But the coolest thing is what Becky made with the helicopter remote!

... the ghosts are attached to the helicopters

... the ghosts spin like crazy in circles overhead!

All my new scares worked perfectly! So then I continued to feed Donna stories of the haunted gym!

And the worst part is, the ghosts stole all of our monsters! I don't know what they'll do NEXT!

totally buying it!

165

"'And so, gentle readers, I never would have believed it if I didn't see it myself! *The old gym really is haunted!* Lights turning on and off! Ghostly apparitions! And all of Desmond's monsters and effects completely disappeared!'"

Becky stares at the newspaper for a minute as if she could change the words with her eyes. Then she slams the pages on the table in front of me.

"Well, that's just great, Desmond!" she explodes. "All the hours of work fixing that place up and you blew it! Now **nobody's** going to want to come to our Haunted Gym! My dad's going to kill you!"

"Yeah, and you're totally letting Keith get away with stealing your monsters!" adds Ricky. "Now he even has the ghost of Clubflubber to blame! And he's going to win best haunted house because everybody's going to be too afraid of ours, and you're going to have to give up scaring!"

Yes! Saved by the robot fart! Or, as most of us know it, that most favorite of all kid sounds: the end-of-day school bell.

The hallways erupt like an exploded anthill as everyone runs to their lockers or out the doors. Ricky, Becky, and I join the river of kids headed to the front hall.

SO YOU GUYS THINK THAT PEOPLE WILL STAY AWAY BECAUSE THEY'RE AFRAID THE OLD GYM IS FULL OF REAL GHOSTS?

Just as they are both about to jump all over me, we round the corner and . . .

# 24 THE NEW THREAT

"Well done, Pucket! Aces! I expect your Haunted Gym is going to be a smashing success! Well done *indeed*!"

I always have to stop and stare when words like that come out of Mr. Needles these days. It's like hearing the Creature from the Black Lagoon sing a lullaby. Totally upside down.

OK, the Joker smile is still a little weird, but I think I'm actually starting to like that guy!

Becky, Ricky, and I continue to push through the crowd around the ticket booth when suddenly, we're all grabbed together from behind—

Don't be fooled by all the time Ms. Ruebbles is in the library . . . judging from that bone-breaking hug, I'd say she's spending just as much time at the gym!

"You guys, I'm just so proud you!" Ms. Ruebbles gushes when she finally releases us from her crushing squeeze. "And I just wanted to let you know how much I appreciate what you're doing for me and the library!"

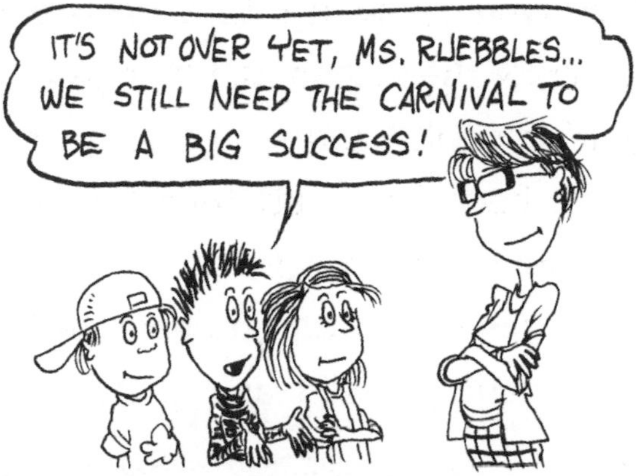
IT'S NOT OVER YET, MS. RUEBBLES... WE STILL NEED THE CARNIVAL TO BE A BIG SUCCESS!

"As far as I'm concerned, you three are the success," she says, and then walks away dabbing her eyes with a tissue.

"Wow," says Ricky. "That's the first time I've ever made a teacher 'happy cry.'"

"You made a teacher 'sad cry'?"

"More like 'frustration cry.' Mr. Shemp in gym. He was trying to explain to me how rotation in volleyball works. I still don't get it."

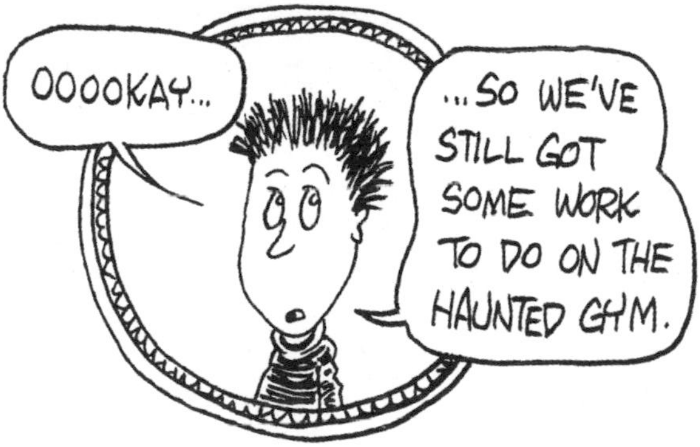
OOOOKAY...
...SO WE'VE STILL GOT SOME WORK TO DO ON THE HAUNTED GYM.

"I'll meet you guys over there at six o'clock. I've got a new idea for the beginning of the ride that I want to sketch out first, OK?"

Ricky and Becky split off for home and I find a nice spot under a nearby tree to work out my new concept. I pull out my spiral notebook of Super Scary Monster Effects and Gross Ideas and start scribbling.

WITH DONNA'S STORY IN THE NEWSPAPER, THIS WILL BE THE PERFECT WAY TO START THE HAUNTED GYM...

Seance Table

candles

Curtains all around

- Medium to conjure spirits
- Speakers for ghost sounds
- lights and projected ghosts

Suddenly, someone steps into my work sunlight . . .

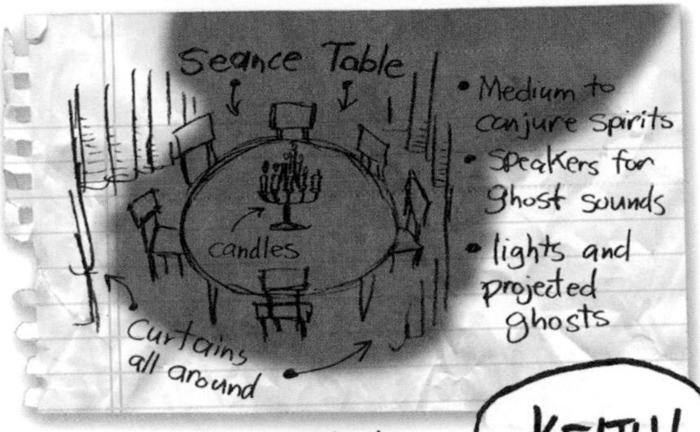
Seance Table
candles
Curtains all around
• Medium to conjure spirits
• Speakers for ghost sounds
• lights and projected ghosts

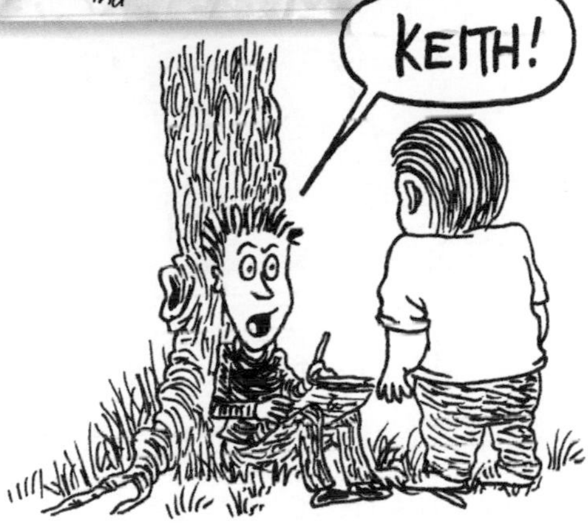
KEITH!

"Looks like you figured out a way to make all those missing monsters turn into a news story," he says. "You're smarter than I thought."

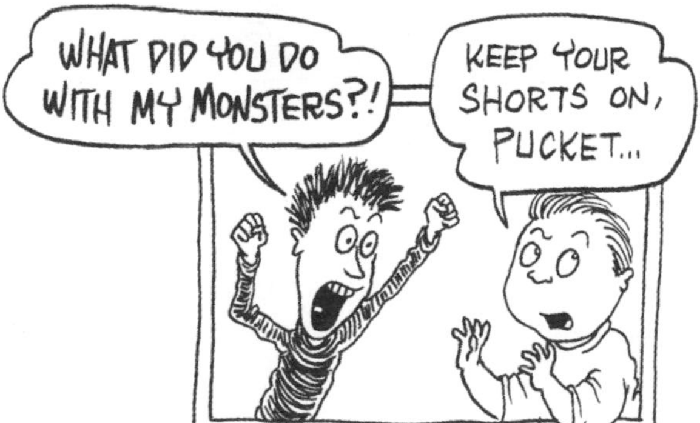
WHAT DID YOU DO WITH MY MONSTERS?!
KEEP YOUR SHORTS ON, PUCKET...

"I'm going to give your monsters back. You're beating me without them. I don't need them anymore."

"It was stuck all by itself in the back of that shed. It's not really a monster at all, Desmond. Just a ghostly thing . . . you'll never miss it!"

"Which ONE?!"

Keith reaches into his pocket and pulls out a small walkie-talkie.

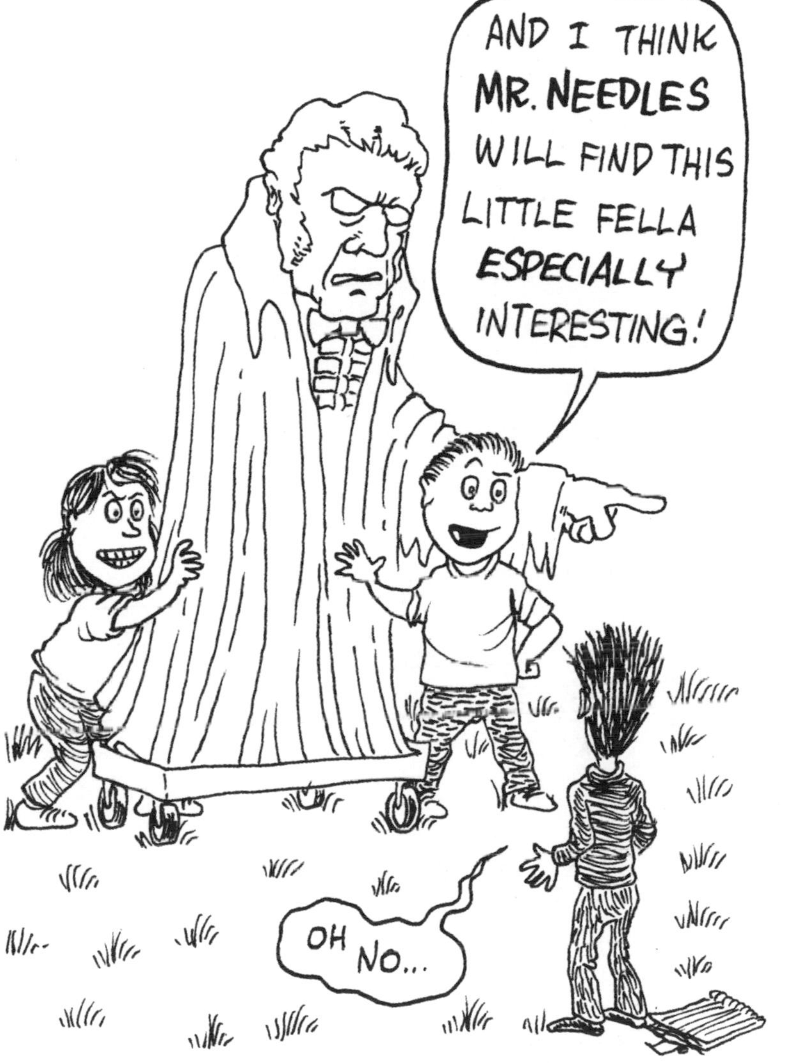
AND I THINK MR. NEEDLES WILL FIND THIS LITTLE FELLA ESPECIALLY INTERESTING!
OH NO...

# 25 RETURN OF THE GHOST

THE GHOST OF
J.J. CLOVERFIELD...
PRETTY CLEVER,
PUCKET...

"You know, for the longest time I couldn't figure out how you did it . . . how you got Principal Needles to change overnight. And then I met *this* guy—"

"Keith, you can't—"

"Can't what? Show Principal Needles your little ghost? Expose your whole plan to trick him? Well, now, that *is* an idea . . ."

"Keith, you *know* what will happen if Mr. Needles sees this," I say. "He'll go nuts! And he'll definitely shut down the Carnival of Horrors! And our rides!"

PROBABLY RIGHT...

...PROBABLY GO RIGHT BACK TO BEING THE OLD NEEDLES.

THAT'S WHAT I'M AFRAID OF!

"Yes, that *would* be terrible," Keith says. "If the carnival is canceled, then you'd have to give back all the ticket money and Ms. Ruebbles will lose her job! We really need to keep Principal Needles from seeing your ghost, don't you think, Pucket?"

"Whoa, buddy, personal space," Keith says, pushing me back. "It's not blackmail when we *both* want something . . ."

"And I can make Desmond's dream come true, just by keeping my mouth shut and hiding our little ghost of J.J. Cloverfield!"

# 26 DESMOND'S LAST STAND

Did you ever see a sad seventh grader sitting on a giant pile of monsters? Well, now you can say that you have.

Yep, I finally got my monsters back from Keith. Well, all except one. The most important one, as it turns out. And now I feel like a prizefighter in one of those old boxing movies . . .

Throw the fight. Kiss the canvas. For Keith.

"Desmond, you know I'm your best friend forever," Ricky says. "But sometimes even I don't know what you're talking about."

Ricky and Becky have met me back at the old gym like they said they would. Even Tina shows up, to help finish our ride. And they find me sitting on this mound of monsters mumbling about boxing movies.

"Guys, I really appreciate all your hard work on the Haunted Gym. But it's over. Finished. Done."

"No, Becky!" I cut her off. "We're finished! Keith found the J.J. Cloverfield ghost! Now if we don't do what he wants, Keith says he's going to spill the beans to Mr. Needles!"

"Wait . . . what does Keith want?" Ricky asks.

"And then he'll be crowned King of All Scare Rides and I'll . . . I'll have to give up scaring."

All three faces stare back at me, looking like they just heard that they have to report to school on Saturdays from now on.

"So, let him tell Mr. Needles!" Becky shouts.

"Yeah," adds Ricky. "And *we'll* tell Mr. Needles exactly *everything* that Keith—"

WE **CAN'T**, YOU GUYS! MR. NEEDLES WILL GO BACK TO HIS OLD SOUR SELF IF HE FINDS OUT ABOUT OUR FAKE GHOST!

"Then he'll shut down both the rides or cancel the whole Carnival of Horrors! And we won't be able to raise money for the library or Ms. Ruebbles! Did you forget? That's what this is all about!"

"Jeez, my dad is going to freak when he finds out all his work here was for nothing!" Becky yells in my face, giving me a shove. "And you're already on his list, Desmond!"

"Me?! This isn't my fault! Keith outsmarted all of us!"

"You're just a big chicken," Ricky yells at the other side of my head. "You backed right down! I say we go take care of Keith ourselves, right now!"

With that, Ricky lunges for my spiral notebook of Super Scary Monster Effects and Gross Ideas.

Before I can figure out what Ricky means by that, we're all grappling for the book. Becky, too, and the pages start flying everywhere.

It's Tina. I forgot she's standing there.

"So the Carnival of Horrors is Saturday," she says, totally ignoring our scuffle. "That gives us two days to come up with our new lame-o Haunted Gym."

"What are you talking about, Tina?" I ask, pulling my foot out from Ricky's armpit. "Lame is lame. It doesn't take any time to do."

"You're not thinking about this thing the right way, Cousin Eerie."

"Wait, how can we—" I start to ask, but Tina is already up and looking closely at the pile of monsters.

"C'mon, you slugs!" she shouts. "We've got some changes to make and little time to make them!"

# 27 SHOWTIME!

It's Saturday and the Cloverfield Junior High Carnival of Horrors is in full-on beast mode.

I, of course, am dressed in my finest horror-wear:

Me, frightfully
Attired

Homemade
fangs

Skull
cane

Top Hat
with skull
band

Vest with
Zombie head
pattern

Specially
designed
bat wing
bow tie

The place is packed with kids, pre-school through high school senior, and it looks like we're going to raise a ton of cheddar today! At least I hope so. I'm counting on the usual Friday allowance kid-payday.

I drew this map so you can see everything:

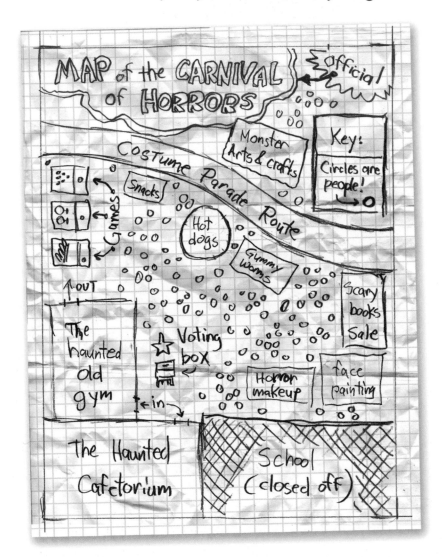

And right now, the most important thing to me is that voting box!

There it is, sitting between my ride and Keith's ride, with Mr. Needles nearby to make sure the voting stays fair. Mr. Needles, by the way, is especially festive today in his pink striped suit, yellow-and-green-diamond vest, and bright orange bow tie. He looks like a big bowl of Lucky Charms. Kind of out of place at a Carnival of Horrors, but he's smiling, so I don't ask any questions.

Ricky and Becky are inside the old gym running the show. I figure it's time to check in.

I bolt over to the ride's exit and stand out of sight, to see if I can spy some reaction.

And then others start pouring out with the same complaints. Well, that's what we expected from the older kids. Now let's just hope that Tina can hold up her end of this plan!

"Pretty soon my Haunted Cafetorium will be voted best and I'll be crowned King of All Scare Rides and *you* . . ."

"Yeah, and I heard about your Haunted Cafetorium," I say. "Did you know some of the little kids are coming out of there crying?"

GUITLY AS CHARGED!
I HAVE TO ADMIT
I **DO** LOVE SCARING
THE LITTLE THINGS!

"Their sweet, tiny faces are just so cute when they're screaming in total fear! See you at the winner's podium, Pucket!"

Keith walks off laughing and I stumble over to the snack stand to drown my sorrows in a sour gummy worm scary-cherry punch. Now I'm starting to panic! What if Keith wins? How can I give up scaring?! I just renewed my membership in the Fangs-of-the-Month Club! This could be a total disaster!

Three hours and seven gummy worm punches later, the loudspeaker crackles to life:

"First things first," blares Mr. Needles's important principal voice from the gray speakers above. "I want to thank everyone for coming and making this year's Carnival of Horrors a big success!"

Maybe it's that seventh gummy worm punch, but my stomach is dancing the Macarena.

And like all great American winners, I immediately celebrate by throwing up on my shoes.

# 28 THE GREAT KEITH MELTDOWN

"I'm the one who should be mad, Keith," I say. "My mom just bought me these shoes!"

"Let him go, Keith!" Tina shouts. "It was me. Your sister. It was my idea."

Keith thinks for a second. "You mean the 'It's a Small World' ride?"

"And why do you hate 'It's a Small World' so much?" Tina asks.

"I hate it because it's full of happy, singing kids and bright colors and dancing flowers and—*BLEH*!"

"Yeah, right, it's sweet and pretty and tons of people love it! And it also happens to be *my* favorite ride, by the way!"

"We figured you'd make an over-the-top super-fright ride that would be too much for the little kids," I chime in. "So Tina got the idea to turn the Haunted Gym into a lame-o kiddie ride."

"And the kids love it," finishes Tina.

She then pulls out a small stack of paper and hands them to Keith.

"I've been walking around the carnival handing these out to parents all day."

"I guess you can say we made our own haunted 'It's a Small World,'" I add. "So we ended up getting the votes from all the little kids *and* their parents!"

"It's pretty cool," I say. "C'mon, I'll show you!"

Keith, Tina, and I push through the crowd and enter the old gym from the back way, behind the scenes. Then we climb the bleachers to get an overhead view.

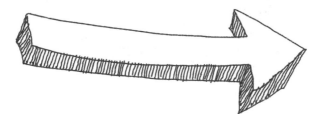

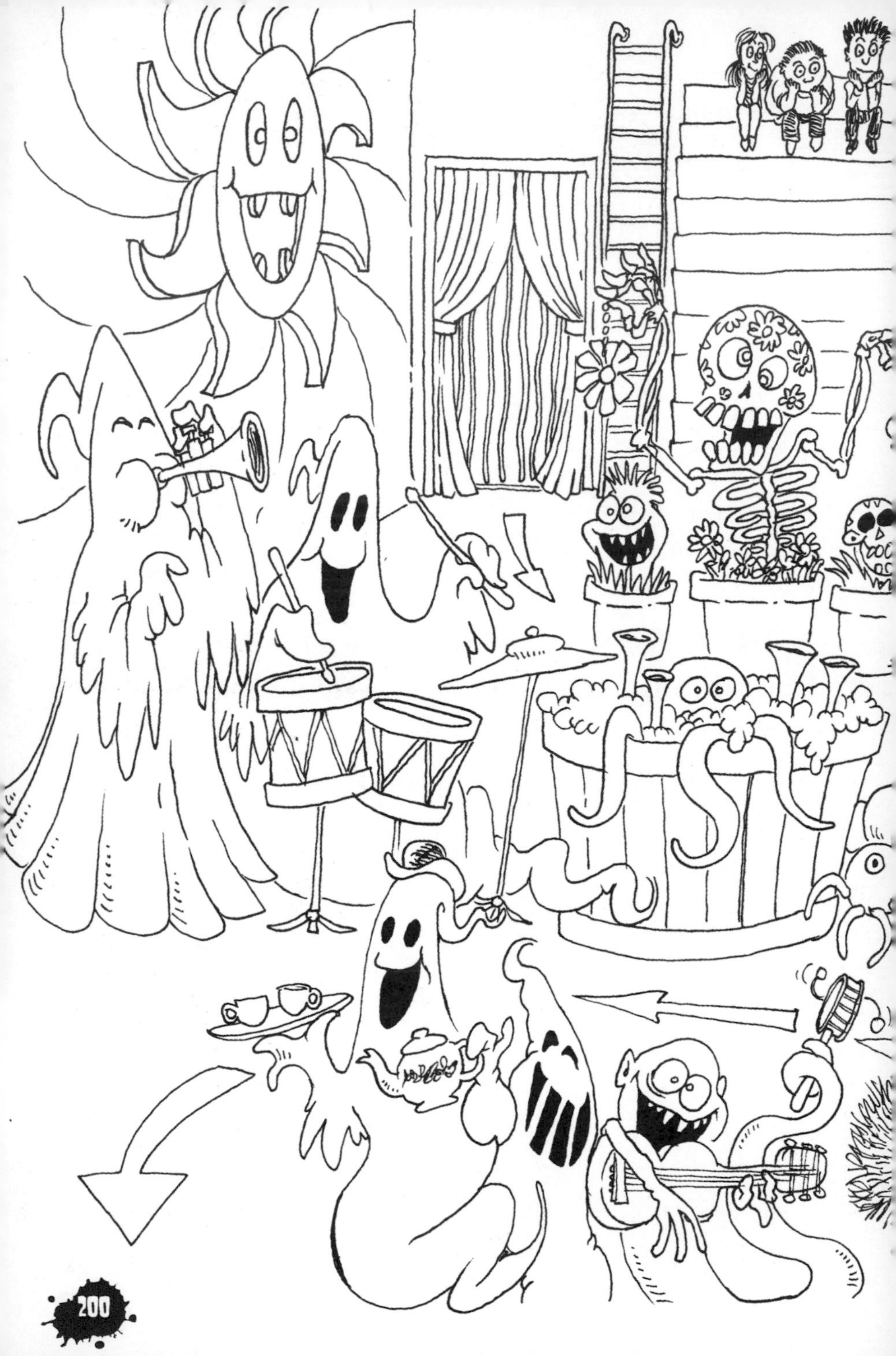

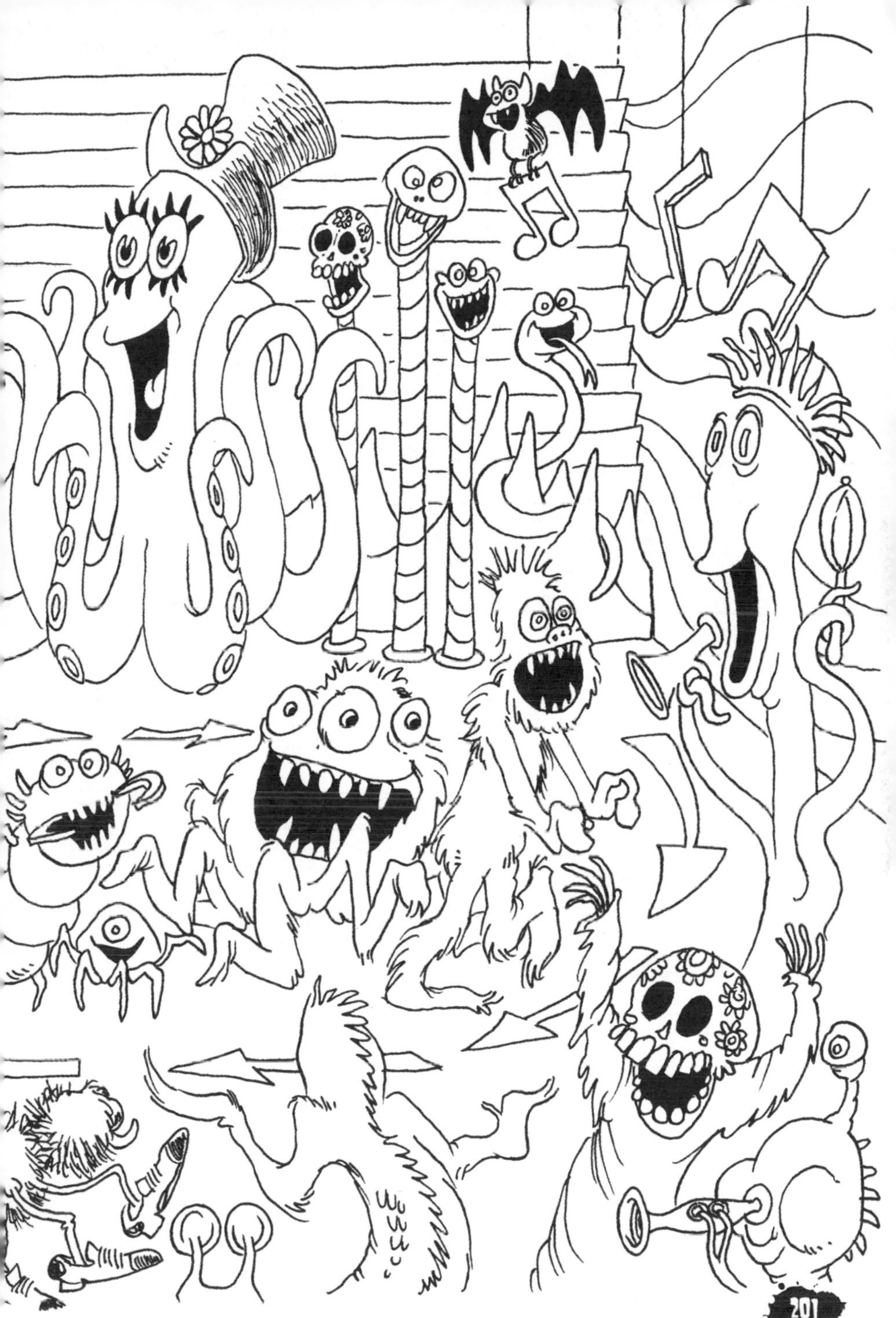

"We spent the last two days turning my monsters into goofy versions of themselves," I say. "Then Ricky added the silly music and it came together. I'm totally surprised that it worked!"

Keith stops suddenly and looks right into my face.

Wait, I've seen that before . . . that's the little walkie-talkie that Keith used for—

Holy crud! Maybe there's still time to stop this—

I scramble over Keith and past Tina, then I'm down the bleachers and out the door in three steps. I dart through the maze of kids and parents, who all seem to be looking at something. I burst through the edge of the crowd and see that I'm . . .

# 29 THE NEEDLES I NEVER KNEW

Oh, no.

This is it.

The moment I was hoping would never happen is happening.

Cinderella's coach is about to turn back into a big, fat, ugly pumpkin.

Suddenly, I feel Ricky, Becky, and Tina crowd in around me. Except for the distant musical pounding of "Monster Mash," the whole carnival is suddenly quiet. And then Keith steps forward.

Still nothing from Mr. Needles, who continues to stare gape-mouthed at the ghostly statue. Like one of those amusement park garbage cans.

"I say he should be disqualified from the Best Ride contest, and I should be crowned King of All Scare Rides!"

That's all we can stand, and we start arguing with Keith about who deserves to win and why he's such a creep and then suddenly—

And then we hear a sound. A low, hissing noise, like air escaping from a blow-up bed. It's coming from between the hands covering Mr. Needles's face.

Is he . . . crying?

No . . . no, I think he's . . . he's . . .

Now there's a rusty laugh that doesn't get out much!

"My dear Mr. Pucket," Mr. Needles says, gripping me by both shoulders. "My very dear, dear sweet Mr. Pucket! What a rapscallion you are!"

Oookaaaaayyyy . . . Is that even a word?!

"Ah, excellent! I know the perfect place for him in my office! Maybe even holding the American flag—"

"And how stupid do you think I am, Mr. Schimsky?"

The four of us stand there staring at Mr. Needles, the same look of shock on all our faces.

"So, you knew it was me and Becky and Ricky the whole time?" I ask. "And you weren't mad?"

"Now, to be sure, I was mad at the time," Mr. Needles continues. "And that night, I immediately went back to the school to start the paperwork to have you expelled!"

"But in the car ride over, I started to think . . ."

"And when I got to the school, instead of heading to my office, I went to the library."

"So I decided to research Mr. J.J. Cloverfield, founder of Cloverfield Junior High . . .

"All night long, I pored over the many books and newspaper stories, digging up everything I could find about the man I so admired.

"And you know what? He was kind. He was supportive. He was encouraging, especially to creative students. He loved the library and always kept it growing. And the kids loved and respected him. But the biggest thing I discovered that night about J.J Cloverfield . . ."

"And from that moment on, I knew I had to change. I didn't like the old me anymore. I felt sure if I met J.J. Cloverfield in real life, I would be embarrassed about who I was. It was time to become a new Needles!"

I stand there, totally surprised at Mr. Needles's story. "So it wasn't our ghost that made you change?"

"And don't forget the library," says Ms. Ruebbles, who has now joined our little circle. "The place with all the answers!"

"And as long as that place has our favorite librarian," I add with a smile.

But Ms. Ruebbles isn't smiling.

# 30 THE BAD NEWS

"I know you guys all worked so hard to save my job," Ms. Ruebbles says. "And this really was the most successful Carnival of Horrors we ever had . . ."

"But . . . we came up short. I just talked to the person handling all the money we took in today, and it just wasn't enough. I'm so sorry, guys! You really outdid yourselves! Unfortunately, I have no choice but—"

Holy crud! It's the superintendent of schools, Mrs. Badonkus! She bursts into our circle holding two little kids.

"These are my twin grandsons, Mickey and Donald," she exclaims to us all.

"Their names are Mickey and Donald?" Ricky asks.

"Oh, please! My son's a huge Disney fan. Don't get me started!"

She hands the two boys off to Ms. Ruebbles and grabs me by the shoulders.

"Yeah, it came out pretty good," I say. "Too bad it wasn't enough to help Ms. Ruebbles."

Mrs. Badonkus waves me quiet and continues.

"You want to keep it a kiddie monster ride?" I ask.

"No, you silly goose! We're going to make it a kiddie day care!"

"The high school can offer classes in child care training, and with the money the school makes from the day care, we can offer our teachers FREE day care for their kids!"

They all turn and look at me.

My monsters. I'd have to give up my monsters. The monsters that I worked so hard to save.

But they were stuck living in Ricky's grandparents' shed, and if now they can save Ms. Ruebbles's job . . .

A giant cheer goes up and Mr. Needles hoists me up onto his shoulder above the waving crush of people. Suddenly an ear-busting scream cuts through the shouts of the crowd.

Oh, no. It's Keith, who climbs onto a snack table to be heard.

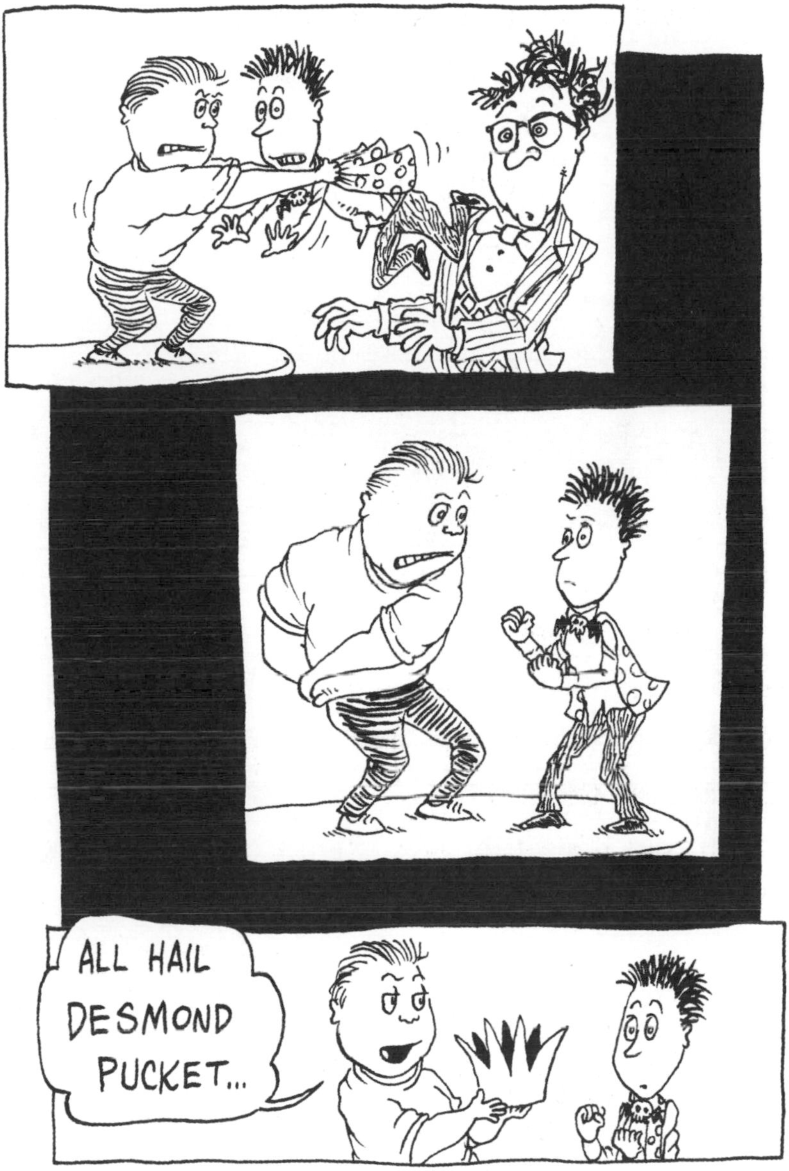
ALL HAIL DESMOND PUCKET...

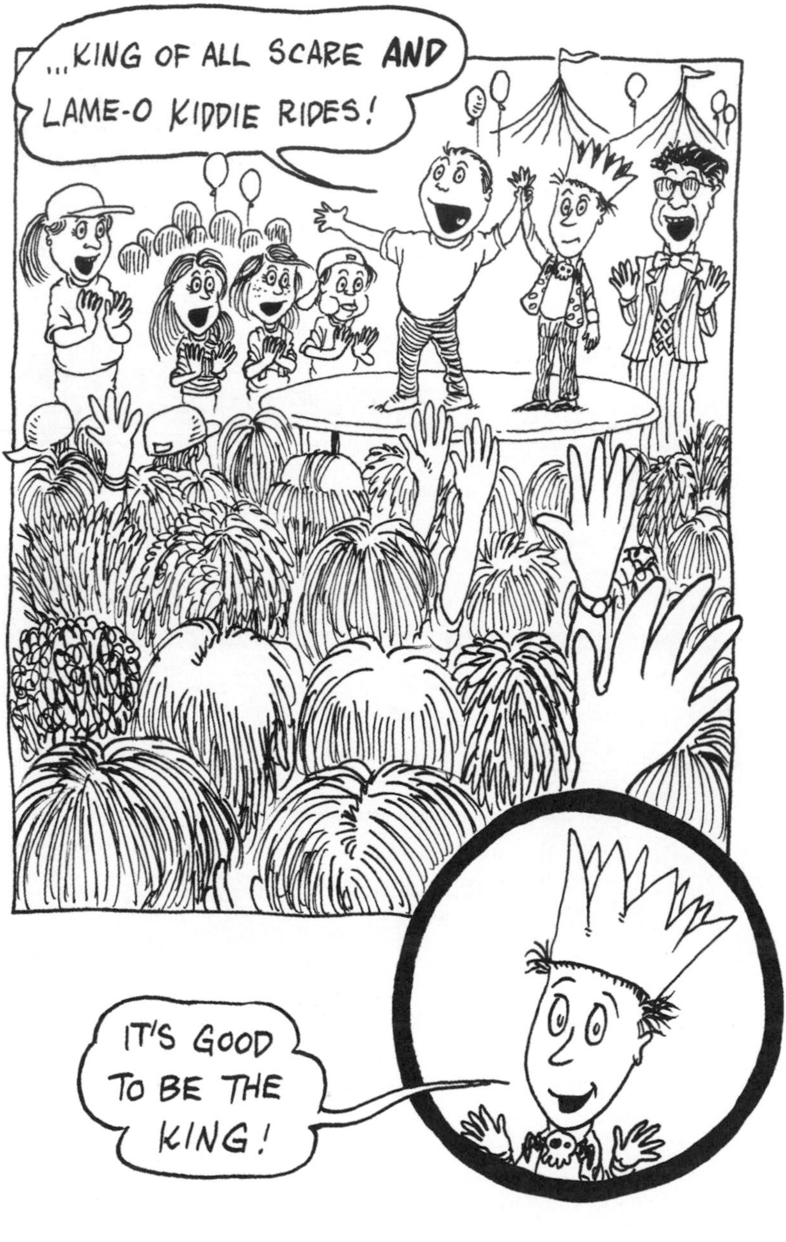
...KING OF ALL SCARE AND LAME-O KIDDIE RIDES!
IT'S GOOD TO BE THE KING!

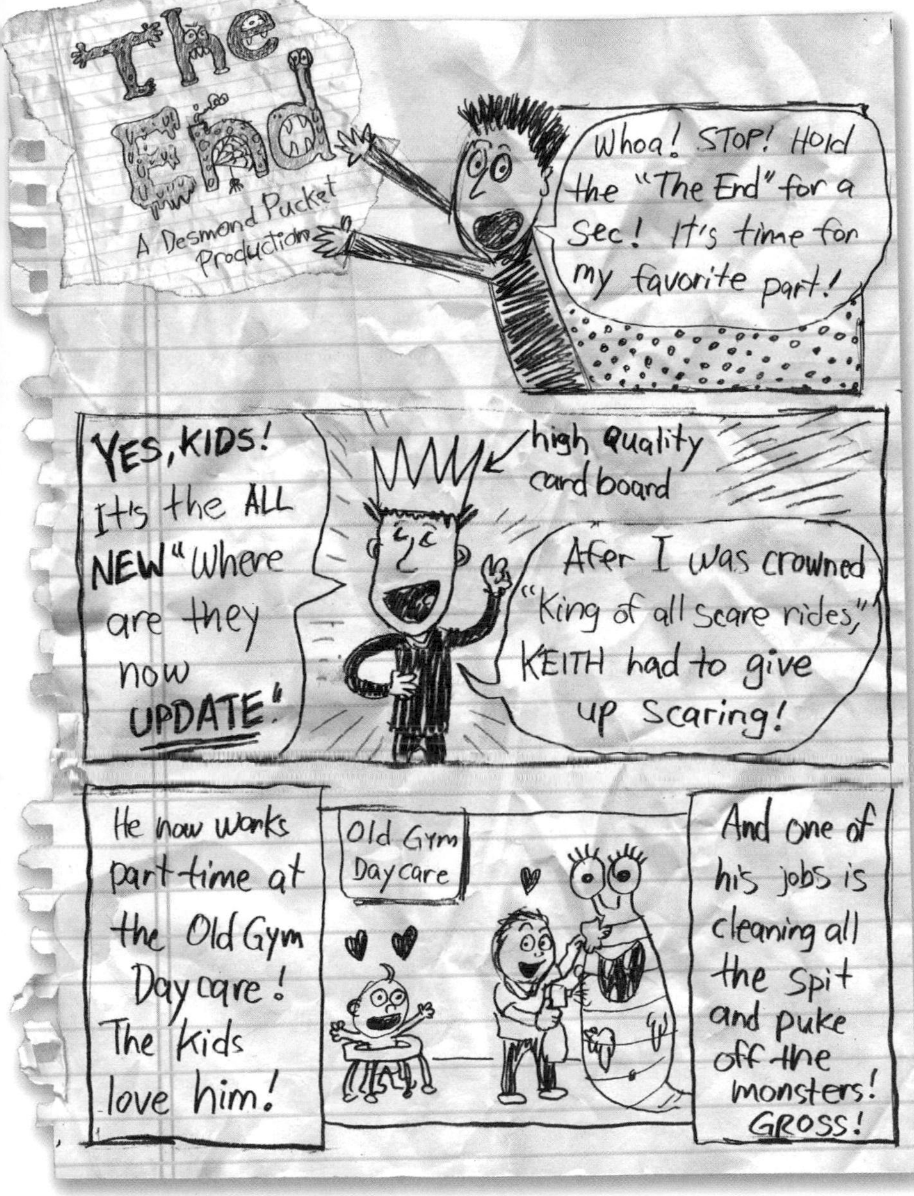
The End
A Desmond Pucket Production
Whoa! STOP! Hold the "The End" for a sec! It's time for my favorite part!
YES, KIDS! It's the ALL NEW "Where are they now UPDATE"!
high quality card board
Afer I was crowned "King of all scare rides," KEITH had to give up Scaring!
He now works part-time at the Old Gym Daycare! The Kids love him!
Old Gym Daycare
And one of his jobs is cleaning all the spit and puke off the monsters! GROSS!

RICKY is still a huge part of my MONSTER MAGICIANS, but he

※1 Audio guy

does have other interests

Right now, he's developing his own fart sound app...

PPFFTTHHBP!!

Hmmmmm... Needs more raspberry.

... it's different fart instruments. Saxaphone, violin, etc. GENIUS!!

MS. RUEBBLES still works in our library! Woo-hoo!

Mr. Pucket, that monster makeup book is overdue!

and she still doesn't cut me any slack.

and it turns out Ms. Ruebbles is a single mom, and now she has a new boyfriend!

Mystery man

GASP! It's MR. NEEDLES And they seem really happy together!

She got him to clip his nosehairs, so that's good.

Speaking about love lives, what about me?

? ? ? ? ? ? ? ?

I really like two girls and now I don't know what to do!

Tina

Becky

TINA is now part of our MONSTER MAGIC team and she's a great addition!

This is brilliant, Tina! Why didn't I think of this?

She has great new ideas, just like the kiddie haunted gym! This of course causes much Becky eye-rolling.

BECKY is still our electronics expert, and she just got a new soldering gun that's pretty sweet!

Awesome protective goggles

She's learning all about robots now! She's the next WAVE of Monster Magician!

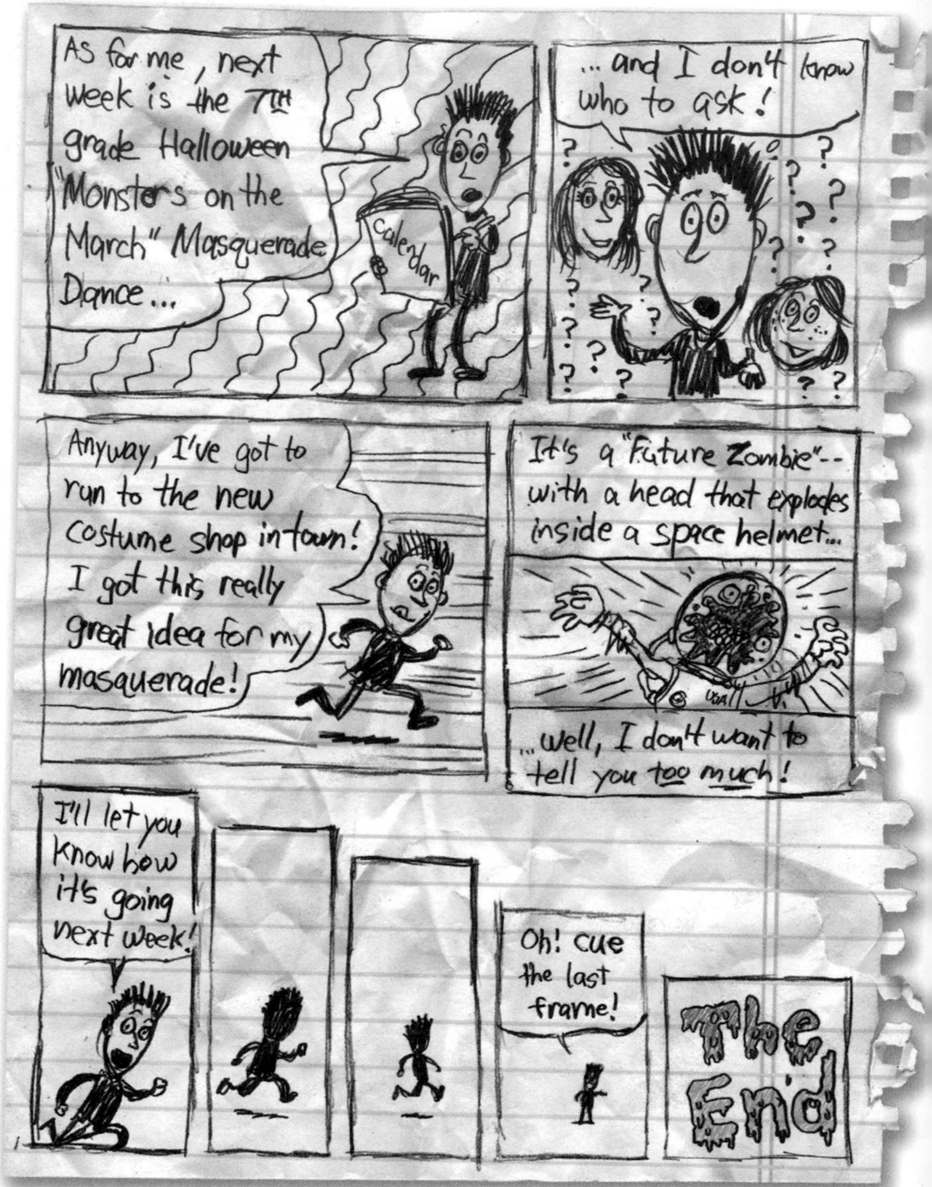

As for me, next week is the 7th grade Halloween "Monsters on the March" Masquerade Dance...
Calendar
...and I don't know who to ask!
Anyway, I've got to run to the new costume shop in town! I got this really great idea for my masquerade!
It's a "Future Zombie"-- with a head that explodes inside a space helmet...
USA
...well, I don't want to tell you too much!
I'll let you know how it's going next week!
Oh! Cue the last frame!
The End

Cloverfield Jr.
Carnival of Horra

# MAKE YOUR OWN MONSTER MAGIC WITH DESMOND'S NOTES

DESMOND'S NOTES
OK, so you're probably wondering...
Me, deep in thought
...How did I make that really AWESOME J.J. Cloverfield GHOST?
Awesome ghost
IT'S Kind of Complicated, so pay close attention!
The making of a ghost
professor pucket
FIRST: I borrowed the J. J. Cloverfield statue from Mr. Needles...
Don't worry, I'll bring it back!

NEXT: I painted the whole head with soapy water.
me
SOAP AND WATER
Why? WAIT, I'll tell you!
Then I placed the head in a box and filled it with a fast-drying, mold-making mix*...
statue head
Mold-o-mix
Box
* You can get this stuff in a hobby or craft store. It's really cool!
...when the mold stuff dried, I peeled it off the head like a glove.
Rubbery mold
Pull
statue head
Now you know why I used the soapy water! To make the mold come off EASY! It's a snap!
Ta-da! A mold of J.T Cloverfield's head!
Then I returned the head to Mr. Needles's office!
Careful! I break easily!

Next:
I poured another fast-drying mixture into the mold! This time, a light-weight, flexible foam.
foam
pour
Mold
Available at the hobby store
We monster magicians like fast-drying stuff because we're always on the move!
After it dried and I pulled it out of the mold... the perfect head of J.J. Cloverfield!
light-weight foam version
Then I carved the inside out so I could move the mouth like a puppet.
Then I brought it all together!
ghost hand
white sheet
me
Becky
ghost hand
tripod
The total J.J. CLOVERFIELD GHOST!
So now You know! It's our secret!

# WELCOME TO DESMOND'S SNOT FACTORY

Here's what you need:

Rubber cement

Waxed paper

① lay out waxed paper on a clean, clear surface.

② Using rubber cement, create "chicken leg" shapes by painting and dripping. Let DRY!

thin here
wide here

③ Once they dry, peel up the shapes and mold into "snotty" look.

Molding

leave a flat end at the top.

④ Stick the flat end under your nose (not **IN** your nose) and go gross someone out ➝

Anybody got a tissue?

DESMOND'S SCARES FOR HALLOWEEN TRICK OR TREATERS!
screen
This works best with a front door that has a screen on top like this.
But if you have a door like this, I'll show you at the end how to make that work, too!
1
On HALLOWEEN NIGHT, Remove the screen!
Trust me, nobody will even know it's missing!

② Prepare yourself with your favorite Halloween Scare costume...
I prefer a full-head latex rubber number.
③ Hide on the inside of the door, below the open window space.
Hiding behind lower door INSIDE
Snicker!
④ Wait for Trick or Treaters.
Knock Knock Knock
⑤ Pop out and let the Scares RIP!
GAHH
SPECIAL NOTE: If you have a full screen door, remove the screen and cover the bottom half with foam core.
door
Foam core is like cardboard, and it's cheap to buy!
Styrofoam center

DESMOND'S MONSTERS OF MOVIELAND
COOL FUN FACTS!
I love old monster movies, and here are some awesome things I learned about how they were made!
NOW SHOWING
"MYSTERIOUS ISLAND" (1961)
Really cool giant monster crab scene!
The animated puppet was made from a real crab! And the crab they used for close-ups ended up being the animator's dinner!
Animated by Ray Harryhausen, a REAL monster magician!
"Phantom of the Opera" (1925)
Lon Chaney, the man of a thousand faces, used WIRES to hold his nose up to look like a skull!
Lon Chaney
Nose pinned up

thin wires
Nose
Lon Chaney
And Lon Chaney's son, Lon Chaney Jr., was also an actor...
He played the famous WOLF MAN monster!
"The Wolf Man" (1941)
Lon Chaney Jr.
"Creature from the Black Lagoon" (1954)
After they finished filming the movies, the creature costume was tossed into the garbage...
TRASH
TRASH
Movie Studio
... a janitor found the monster mask and rescued it, giving it to his son to use as a Halloween costume!
TRICK or Treat
Eventually the costume was discovered and is now being displayed!

Make sure you're caught up on all of
Desmond's monster magic adventures!

Andrews McMeel Publishing
a division of Andrews McMeel Universal
1130 Walnut Street, Kansas City, Missouri 64106

www.andrewsmcmeel.com

16 17 18 19 20 SDB 10 9 8 7 6 5 4 3 2 1

Paperback ISBN: 978-1-4494-7409-6

Hardcover ISBN: 978-1-4494-6628-2

Library of Congress Control Number: 2015951474

Made by:
Shenzhen Donnelley Printing Company Ltd.
Address and place of production:
No. 47, Wuhe Nan Road, Bantian Ind. Zone,
Shenzhen China, 518129
1st Printing— 11/23/2015

**ATTENTION: SCHOOLS AND BUSINESSES**
Andrews McMeel books are available at quantity discounts with bulk purchase for educational, business, or sales promotional use. For information, please e-mail the Andrews McMeel Publishing Special Sales Department: specialsales@amuniversal.com.

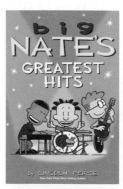